'I'm a film director, not a welfare officer!'

As Thaddeus growled, the warmth of his breath caressed Jenny's cheek.

'If you can't stand the heat, stay out of the kitchen,' he finished angrily, and then raked his hand through his hair in a gesture of impatience as he noted the defiant toss of her head.

'It's not the heat of the kitchen, it's the chef I can't stand,' she retorted angrily, her eyes flashing with hostility.

Dear Reader

Whatever the weather this summer, come with us to four places in the sun. In this collection, we offer you the romance you love – with a dash of the exotic. . .the hazy heat and shimmering sands of Tunisia. . .the colourful glamour of Acapulco Beach. . .the tropical beauty of Indonesia. . .the timeless mystique of Egypt. A magical tour of sensual delight, with four happy endings along the way! Something sultry from Mills & Boon. . .

The Editor

Catherine O'Connor was born and has lived all her life in Manchester, where she is a happily married woman with five demanding children, a neurotic cat, an untrainable dog and a rabbit. She spends most of her time either writing or planning her next story, and without the support and encouragement of her long-suffering husband this would be impossible. Though her heroes are always wonderfully handsome and incredibly rich, she still prefers her own loving husband.

Recent titles by the same author:

DANGEROUS DOWRY
YESTERDAY'S PASSION

THE DEVIL'S CAPTIVE

BY
CATHERINE O'CONNOR

MILLS & BOON LIMITED
ETON HOUSE   18-24 PARADISE ROAD
RICHMOND   SURREY   TW9 1SR

*First published in Great Britain 1993
by Mills & Boon Limited*

© Catherine O'Connor 1993

*Australian copyright 1993
Philippine copyright 1993
This edition 1993*

ISBN 0 263 77986 6

*Set in Times Roman 10 on 12 pt.
93-9307-54651 C*

Made and printed in Great Britain

CHAPTER ONE

THADDEUS'S cool blue eyes flickered critically over her and Jenny felt conscious of the disorderly figure she must present. She normally dressed with keen perfection, always projecting the right professional image. Her hair, which usually was kept in a severe but neat style, had been released from its tight plait for extra comfort and fell in a riot of untidy tresses across her back. The wind had added to her dishevelled appearance, making her look like a dizzy schoolgirl. She began to rummage in her bag for a hairband but the host of papers she had stuffed inside fell over the floor, scattering everywhere. She heard him mumble a curse at her clumsiness and flushed again. It was so unlike her; she was normally so cool, so in control.

She glanced up as she knelt on the floor frantically shoving the papers back into their folder. She could see the sparks of fire sparking in the cold depths of his Prussian blue eyes and she felt a bubble of anger inside. He hadn't even the manners to help her, she thought angrily as she stood to face him. She knew she was breathless and her heart was thudding uncontrollably in her chest. She swallowed the rising lump of fear in her throat as she caught the animal strength of the man, his temper barely leashed, his eyes now like shards of ice searing her soul.

'The schedules,' he said abruptly through sharp white teeth, reminding Jenny of a snarling dog. She felt a

5

trickle of fear down her spine; she had never liked dogs, she thought grimly, waiting for him to say more to explain his anger. He remained silent, his face dark and forbidding, not offering any more information, as if he had expected her to know what was wrong. He waited, his gaze locking her into immobility, and the tension between them increased with every passing moment. His mouth was a grim, uncompromising line, his sharp features seeming chiselled in marble, and just as cold and hard. Jenny's mind raced. She had done the schedules, she knew that. They were all typed up and ready—she had checked them herself, she thought frantically.

'The schedules are all up to date,' she retorted firmly, irritated by his arrogance and the increasing fear he was arousing in her. Her voice betrayed none of the niggling doubts that were beginning to grow in the back of her mind, as she faced him with determination.

Thaddeus looked at her slowly and she felt her pulse quicken at his inspection. His eyes travelled over her body, not missing a dip or a curve. Jenny allowed herself a secret smile. It did not seem that long ago that she had no figure at all—well, not one that any man would take an interest in! Fury and contempt were apparent in every line of his face, and his eyebrows drew together in a frown, drawing attention to the dark depths of his cold stare.

Again Jenny was conscious of her appearance; it was so at odds with her usual business image. She tucked her hair behind her ears, revealing the gentle softness of her face, a perfect oval with a light sprinkling of freckles across the bridge of her nose which were complemented by the warm glow of her hazel eyes. She knew she looked bad today—she needed rest; she felt tired out and her hair was in need of a trim.

He looked her up and down once more and Jenny felt herself growing increasingly more annoyed at her own behaviour. What did it matter to her, his impression of her? she thought. A flush of red brightened her cheeks yet she refused to let herself be intimidated any further, so she kept her eyes firmly fixed on him, silently counting to ten in an attempt to relax.

'The schedules are up to date but all in the wrong order!' he roared, flinging the papers in to Jenny's stunned face. 'I've two actors here whom I shan't be using till next week and thanks to you the three I need today have taken a fishing trip.'

The shock of having a pile of papers thrown at her caused Jenny to step back in alarm, allowing them to fall like confetti around her feet. She watched them cascade to the floor, in a dreamlike trance as she forced herself to remain calm, refusing to respond to his anger with her own temper. She threw back her head, her eyes now blazing in defiance, and clenched her fists tightly at her sides as she struggled to control her growing annoyance.

Her angry stare met Thaddeus's, locking them both into an angry immobility that neither one was willing to break first. The silence and tension was welling up between them till it was almost palpable. He continued to stare at her, those cold, angry eyes sparking with unspent anger.

'Are you sure?' she asked calmly, amazing herself that she could disguise so well the turmoil she felt inside. She saw the flash of annoyance cross his face. His eyebrows rose first, and then a frown of amazement furrowed his brow.

'I am not in the habit of making mistakes, Miss Collins,' he said tightly, obviously incredulous at her audacity that she should even question him.

Jenny winced at the deliberate gibe at her and bent down to retrieve the papers, pushing them back into some semblance of order. The action gave her time to adjust quickly so she could maintain her calm façade despite the provocation.

'Let's check before we jump to hasty conclusions,' she said sharply, convinced that she was right.

He gave her a look of disgust, and bit back angrily, 'I have checked and, unlike you, double checked, and I'm telling you the schedule is in the wrong order.'

His voice had risen an octave with every word and he was now just keeping it from roaring. Jenny paid no heed to him, too busy sifting through the papers. Her agile mind could see no mistake. Then she quickly checked the papers again. There had been changes. She closed her eyes to blot out the reality of the situation. She swallowed nervously, but knowing something was wrong seemed to only increase her unease. Her eyes shot open and she stood in front of him, taking in the angry contempt etched on his face.

'Well?' snapped Thaddeus, viewing Jenny with a frown that unnerved her, and he stepped towards her. That animal grace was still there in his movements, a savage, predatory look on his face. Jenny subconsciously registered the dangerous, threatening way he was approaching and instinctively stepped back. Yet her gaze remained fixed on him warily, watching his every move. He stepped still closer, till she could catch the masculine musky scent of his aftershave, and looked down at her, devilish lights flashing now in his eyes.

She felt her pulse leap at his proximity, her sight level with the taut broadness of his hard-muscled chest and strong column of his tanned neck.

'I'm sorry, there does appear...' she mumbled, suddenly aware of the disturbing electricity that was being transmitted between them. She knew he was angry, and his temper would no doubt only increase when she told him who was at fault. Yet instinctively Jenny also knew there was more than just anger between them, and that was even more frightening.

'Sorry? Sorry?' he mocked, a dry, humourless laugh echoing around the set. 'Well, I suppose that's something, but your apology is hardly of any value.'

His voice was hard and scathingly sarcastic. Jenny felt herself colour; she couldn't believe her ears; the sheer audacity of the man was overwhelming.

'Mr Clarke,' she interrupted smartly, her voice sharp and cutting, 'you seem to be under the impression that the fault lies with me.' He shot her a flash of surprise, and Jenny continued, 'The schedules I was given and consequently distributed are all correct.'

She paused, enjoying the changing expression on his face. 'However, the filming has since been altered, which is hardly my fault. I was not informed of the changes,' she added forcefully, hoping that her gibe would hit home.

For a moment he was silent; his gaze flickered across her and Jenny immediately straightened. She was proud of her body now; the shape she had worked so hard to achieve gave her a confidence she hadn't had before. Thaddeus considered her words.

'I changed the filming details, but I sure as hell passed them on——'

'Not to me, Mr Clarke,' she interrupted him smartly again, but she still wanted to shield the unfortunate individual who had obviously forgotten to tell her. Not that she could blame whoever it was. The workload had been huge, and whose fault was that? she thought irritably, suddenly feeling weary and exhausted.

'An oversight, I'm sure,' she continued. 'The workload has been tremendous. We have all been working flat out—not that you care...' She stopped abruptly, realising she had gone too far as two strong hands fell heavily on her shoulders, catching her in a fierce, angry grip.

'I'm a director, not a welfare officer!' he growled, his fingers sinking into her soft flesh. The warmth of his breath caressed her cheek. 'If you can't stand the heat, stay out of the kitchen,' he finished angrily, giving her shoulders a shake. He raised his hand to rake it through his thick, dark hair in a gesture of impatience as he noted the defiant toss of her head.

'It's not the heat of the kitchen, it's the chef I can't stand,' she retorted angrily, her eyes flashing with hostility so that they shone like flares of golden light. He glared at her, yet his mouth quirked a little, betraying his amusement at her quick response. His obvious amusement only upset her even more, and she felt hot pinheads prick till unbidden tears began to come. He turned his back on her, mumbling a curse as he sunk his hands deep into his trouser pockets, his anger still volatile even while he was struggling to control it. Jenny could see that by the very stiffness of his stance. Her heart was racing, causing a painful lump in her chest.

She closed her eyes momentarily, blinking away her tears; she did not want to appear weak—her very career was on the line here and she knew she had to act fast to keep hold of any chance she had of retaining her credibility. She knew he was right: stamina was an essential part of the job.

'I'm going to lose two days' filming at least because of this,' he growled. 'Two whole days!' He snorted in disgust and paced over to the window, looking out on to the waiting rows of film scenery. A sudden sense of defeat seemed to come over him and his shoulders sagged. He leant his head on the cold pane of glass. Jenny stood watching him, full of remorse; filming was a costly business and no director liked using more money than absolutely essential, as it could jeopardise further jobs.

'Where's the fishing trip?' she asked suddenly, breaking into the wall of anger between them. 'I could reach them, tell them to come back,' she offered hurriedly. Jenny knew she was capable of finding the actors; her stubbornness had often helped her to triumph over insurmountable problems. He swung round, his grim expression silencing her immediately, but she stood her ground, confident she could help, matching his disbelief with her own determination to succeed.

'They've gone on a fishing trip to get away from it all. They would hardly have left forwarding addresses,' he snapped as if amazed by her naïveté.

'Well, someone must know where they are,' she countered, determined not to give in despite the look of incredulity on his face. He shrugged his powerful shoulders by way of a reply and she saw some of the tension ease away. He nodded briefly, a measure of relief evident on his hard-boned face.

'Yes,' he drawled, 'you're probably right. Find them—tell them to get back here at once,' he ordered, scanning her briefly with a flicker of approval.

Jenny nodded and scurried away, though she was painfully aware that he carried on watching after her. She could feel his eagle-sharp sight boring into her back and again she felt her heart race. She allowed herself a smile of satisfaction; she liked the effect she had on men now, the interest they took in her shapely figure. Yet there was something about him that made her feel on the defensive. In many ways he was like Paul—tall and dark-haired with a lean-muscled body—but it wasn't the physical aspects that made them seem alike. It was the same obsessiveness, the need to keep on till everything was just perfect, regardless of the emotional costs. She shivered. It was the same cold ruthlessness that had destroyed her love for Paul that she now saw again so clearly mirrored in Thaddeus Clarke.

She had known from the first moment of meeting him that there was going to be trouble between them. He had already acquired a formidable reputation as a perfectionist who never let a shot past until he deemed everything was absolutely correct. He had a very high level of commitment and expected the same from everyone else. Many thought it a privilege to work with him, but not Jenny; she hated men like him, too blinkered to see anything but their own egos.

She had sensed immediately that she and Thaddeus were not going to get on. There was something in the way he looked at her, that very first day, that had put her on her guard. Piercing shafts of light stripped her soul bare and burned her flesh. She also didn't like the gossip that abounded about his personal life. He seemed capable of embarking on a relationship with every passing good-looking female, and Jenny had no intentions of falling for his charm. She had been a foolish victim once before and she was not about to repeat the performance.

She kept her relationship with Thaddeus on purely business lines, never using his first name and always ensuring that she was one jump ahead of him. Jenny knew it annoyed him—she could tell that whenever he spoke to her, his dry, almost mocking voice irritated. Yet the real problems arose once filming began. Jenny was unable to do anything to his satisfaction. He roared like an angry bear at her at every opportunity, and now the mix-up in the schedules was the worst thing ever. Jenny knew she had to find these actors—but where?

She rubbed her forehead wearily and squeezed her eyes shut. She now realised what an impossible task she had taken on.

'Getting anywhere?' a crisp voice clipped, and Jenny opened her eyes, to be confronted once more by Thaddeus's muscular frame leaning casually against the doorframe. Yet the animal strength in his stance made her wary of his laid-back manner. He looked as if he expected her to fail, and it incensed Jenny immediately.

'No,' she answered honestly, 'but I shall.'

'Really?' he queried, his sensuous mouth widening to reveal the brightness of his teeth. He straightened up and entered her little office, dwarfing it even more. 'You seem very confident,' he drawled, briefly scanning the numerous phone directories that were scattered over her desk with a wry smile of amusement.

'Yes, I am,' she replied frostily, turning her attention back to the job in hand to avoid the humorous gleam in his eyes.

'Have you tried Ambleside?' he asked carelessly, ficking through a magazine that lay discarded on her desk. Jenny's head shot up, a frown flickering across her face. She was immediately aware of his change of tone and he knew it.

'Why should I try Ambleside?' she asked, watching him with interest.

He moved back to the door with a purposeful stride, supremely confident, and tossed back over his broad shoulders as he left, 'That's where they told me they were going.' He gave a short laugh as he left and Jenny thumped the desk in angry frustration. He had deliberately kept that piece of information from her, waiting to see if she would tire of searching for them. She glared at his retreating back in silence, refusing to give him the satisfaction of knowing how much he annoyed her.

There were many hotels and boarding houses in Ambleside and Jenny's fingers soon ached; she had telephoned virtually every hotel but to no avail—the actors were nowhere to be found. She was about to give up and admit to Thaddeus that filming would have to be delayed when suddenly she struck lucky.

It took all her powers of persuasion to entice the men away from their cosy retreat but finally she succeeded, and they agreed to be back at the studios by late afternoon. Jenny was delighted; it was a huge weight off her shoulders and she hurried to find Thaddeus to tell him the news.

She finally found him sitting alone, his head bent as he looked at the papers scattered over his desk. The light from the desk cast a warming shadow across his face, softening his sharp features.

Jenny stood watching him with curiosity. The gentle sound of a classical piano piece being played somewhere in the studios filled the room, making the atmosphere strangely tranquil. Then she walked slowly towards him, her neck craning to see what he was looking at with such intent. His interest in it was undeniable, his gaze soft and full of warmth as he studied the photograph.

Jenny stiffened, her own eyes dilating as she caught who he was looking at. The face was instantly recognisable, the dark green eyes filled with unspoken promises, the provocative curl of the full lips teasing and seductive. Jenny felt her stomach plummet. A damp, angry perspiration broke out on her back. Had he discovered her secret?

She swallowed a rising lump of nausea as she too stared at the photograph. His head shot up as he heard her footfall and he scowled. Jenny noticed it at once and unknowingly returned it with one of her own. He straightened himself in the chair and stretched, raising his strong arms high above his head and arching his back like a huge, splendid panther. Then he groaned softly, a deeply sensuous sound from deep within his chest. Jenny watched him in quiet fascination. He was a powerfully built man, his sexuality stirring her despite her attempts to remain immune to him. He lowered his arms in a slow, graceful movement calculated, she felt sure, for maximum effect. He rested his hands back on the desk and looked at her quizzically, his expression slumbrous, and she felt her pulse leap at his appraisal of her.

'Well,' he drawled, his voice dangerously quiet and smoky as he cast her an oblique glance. 'Have you been successful?'

Jenny stood with a composure she did not feel. She felt he was being deliberately provocative. She nodded.

'Yes, I've managed to trace them, and if the roads are clear they should be back by this evening, maybe late afternoon if we're lucky,' she informed him briskly.

'Good,' he said non-committally, his dark eyes unreadable.

'I could have found them sooner if you had told me they had gone to Ambleside,' she said critically, her mouth thinning to a narrow line.

'I forgot.' He laughed, enjoying her discomfort.

'Did you?' she replied, her voice heavy with sarcasm, her sight dropping to the photograph on his desk. She had already noted the sensuous look on his face and knew who had put it there. As if he had read her mind his gaze dropped back to his desk and he looked at the photograph again.

'Recognise her?' Thaddeus asked, oblivious to Jenny's reaction. She nodded dumbly.

'Doesn't everyone?' she admitted bitterly, with a stab of jealousy. 'She's been around long enough,' she added, not realising the bitterness that had entered her tone. Thaddeus looked at her curiously, his mouth appearing to twitch with suppressed laughter.

'Miaow,' he mocked, as he viewed Jenny speculatively. 'You know her?' he asked quizzically. Jenny shifted uncomfortably; he was far too astute. She frowned but didn't answer. It was all in the past and she certainly didn't want it all bringing back.

'Well?' He waited, a trace of impatience in his voice. 'How did you meet her—have you worked together?' He was watching her closely—too closely—and she heard alarm bells ringing in her head.

'I do know her,' she confessed slowly, a dull ache in her heart as she recalled her memories. She was amazed at her composure: her voice was so icy, so emotionless.

'Good,' he rapped out, as he placed the photograph back down carefully. Jenny started.

'Good—why?' she snapped, a sudden *frisson* of panic alerting her, and she stared at Thaddeus, her look demanding a response.

'I hope she will star in my next production. It's a historical piece, and as I hope it will make the big screen I need a couple of big-name stars. She will be ideal along with Pablo Tagore.'

'Pablo Tagore,' she repeated numbly, as if trapped in some terrible nightmare that was slowly closing in around her. She was frozen with horror; her breathing suddenly became choking and her heartbeat turned into rapid palpitations. All colour drained from her face and she felt cold, the cruellest of colds.

The name rang through her mind, screaming through her brain, making her dizzy as her mind became a vortex of images. She felt herself sway and gripped the table for support. She swallowed the rising lump of panic in her throat as she suffocated her feelings and tried to present a calm façade to Thaddeus. It had been a surprise to see Margaret again in that photograph, but not totally unexpected—the rumours about this film and who was to star in it had been floating around for some time—but Pablo—that was another thing entirely.

She watched as Thaddeus flipped open the folder before him and drew out a photograph of Pablo. He was as handsome as ever and somehow the way he smiled made him look alive, as if at any moment he would speak.

A sharp stab of pain seared through Jenny as the past flooded back, jostling for supremacy till all she could see was Pablo's smile, and her heart ached. Thaddeus tapped the photograph thoughtfully, unaware of the impact he was making.

'I think he's just right—he's a natural, and his looks—well, he already looks like a pirate king.' He laughed, a low, deep rumble as his eyes flicked to Jenny's, his mouth suddenly narrowing when he saw the expression on her face. 'What is it? You look sick.'

The abrupt tone of his voice was strangely at odds with his expression, mused Jenny, but she was too busy to care to deeply about that. Her whole body was suddenly alive with fear and anguish. She had been so confident that she was over Pablo, and yet just seeing his picture created havoc.

'No, I'm fine—fine,' she said, a little too quickly as she tried to cover her tracks. Thaddeus scowled as he viewed her with curiosity.

'When are you starting filming?' Jenny asked, hoping that it was soon and that she would be on holiday. The thought of bumping into Pablo was too much to bear. She couldn't face him; she never wanted to see him again. She had given everything to him, nearly her very life, and in return all he gave was pain and sorrow.

'Soon as I've finished this current shoot—which I was hoping to do by next week,' he added pointedly, the sharpness back in his tone. 'Not that we will be using the studios at first; it's mostly on location.'

Jenny nodded, a huge wave of relief sweeping over her, and her breathing becoming settled. 'I'm due for a holiday, so unfortunately I shan't be able to renew my acquaintance with Margaret Miller.' She tried to make her voice light and airy as if the whole thing was of no consequence.

Thaddeus's eyes narrowed to diamond chips, his head shot up, and he gripped Jenny's hand tightly in a firm hold.

'Cancel your holiday,' he snapped angrily. 'I need you on this job.'

His voice was chilling. It held a menace in its firm, threatening tone, too. But Jenny was not about to be intimidated; although she was not going away, she longed for the peace and tranquillity of her country home, especially after the gruelling regime of the last weeks, and nothing and no one could possibly induce her to go on the shoot. And the thought of meeting Pablo was too hard to bear. She definitely would not be going.

'I can't,' she answered back, her voice heavy with conviction. She tried to pull her hand free but struggled fruitlessly against Thaddeus's hard body, the heat of which warmed her own. He shot to his feet, his expression dark and dangerous.

'Can't, or won't?' he demanded through gritted teeth, his grip tightening forcibly on her hand.

'Does it make any difference? The outcome is the same,' she cried, surprised by the determination in her voice. 'I'm due a holiday and I'm taking it. After working for you I deserve it,' she ended pointedly, pulling herself free with an angry twist. She stayed facing him, her face flushed with anger and exertion. The thought of being forced to work alongside Pablo Tagore filled her head till it pounded against her ears.

Thaddeus did not react to her outburst. He viewed her with a disdain that made her shiver after the warm impact of his body next to hers. Jenny suddenly felt very foolish. She had over-reacted because of Pablo, and Thaddeus's look of grim curiosity warned her that she had revealed too much. He was the last person she wanted to know the truth.

'Most people,' he informed her coldly, 'would consider working with me a privilege, and this new venture is a chance in a million.' His lean features were suddenly etched with the subtle grey light of day that was filtering through from the dismal sky through a window.

Jenny stared in disbelief; the man was so insufferably arrogant that she allowed herself a smile. 'Mr Clarke, if you don't mind, I will forgo the honour of working with you for a much needed holiday,' she said, pleased by her coolness. For a moment she wasn't sure who she was most angry with, Pablo or Thaddeus—each of them had wanted to use her for his own aims.

'This isn't only of personal importance to me. It is the first full-length feature film this company has embarked on. I suspect only the best crew will be asked to go,' he informed her, yet his voice was so cutting that the compliment that she was considered good at her job went unnoticed.

'I'm due a holiday and shall be taking it. I was forced to come on this present job because every other PA has been intimately involved with you,' she snapped.

'And you feel left out? You are complaining?' he teased, stroking her arm with his fingertips. Jenny stiffened at his electric touch, a *frisson* of awareness travelling the length of her arm. She drew back, alarmed by her own reaction and angered by his total self-assurance.

'No, Mr Clarke, I'm not complaining. However, if I were to make a complaint, it would be more likely to concern sexual harassment,' she returned frostily.

He sat back in his seat, a pretend look of mock horror on his face.

'Now really, Miss Collins, I do think that's a case of wishful thinking. We have nothing more than a professional relationship and I hope it will remain as such,' he added, with a devilish delight that warned her that he was not being entirely truthful.

'I can assure you, Mr Clarke, that the only response I could ever want from you would be one of professional respect.' Jenny's smile widened even further as she caught the flicker of anger flit across his face.

'It suits you.'

'Pardon?'

'A smile—you should do it more often,' he observed, his sensual mouth widening itself into a smile that seared her soul. Jenny felt herself colour and hated herself for it. He made her feel gauche and she wasn't at all flattered by his sexist remark, she reminded herself as her own smile began to widen till the dimples in her cheeks were clearly visible.

'I haven't had much to smile about just recently,' she retorted briskly, pleased when her obvious gibe hit home. He raised his eyebrows, allowing another glimmer of amusement.

'I see,' he said sagely, his smile still tugging at the corners of his wide mouth. 'Then let me make amends. Hungry?'

'Pardon?' she snapped. He knew nothing of her past, so he was just making a polite enquiry, and she hated herself for still being so sensitive to her problem with food, but she lived in constant fear that it would return.

'I presume you spent your lunch hour chasing up our lost actors, therefore I suggest we eat now. Filming will carry on till quite late tonight and you look quite pale.'

Jenny stood transfixed; had her reaction to Pablo been so clearly seen? She knew the answer, and that was yet another reason why she would find it impossible to do this job. The last thing she wanted was for everyone to know how very silly she had been. Maybe she was being too hard on herself: she had been very young at the time. But her secret was too painful to share with anyone.

Thaddeus didn't wait for Jenny to reply; with agility he grabbed her hand and escorted her to the door with a firmness that brooked no arguments. Jenny, with a little difficulty, fell in step with his long strides, casting a glance at his handsome profile as she did so. She knew he must have an ulterior motive. Thaddeus Clarke was not the type to make amends—he was a law unto himself. She was not going to fall victim again to that type of calculating male, she reminded herself grimly. She had been used once before and no doubt if Thaddeus knew the truth he would use her again. Maybe he'd already found out, she mused, casting another oblique glance at his profile.

Thaddeus was far too handsome, she thought. His features lacked the classical proportions that Paul's had had, but somehow it made him even more handsome. He looked more like a man—a mature man, rugged and experienced. There was no doubt that Thaddeus Clarke had experience. She had seen him in action over the last few weeks and watched him in amazement. He was clever, the way he flirted outrageously with the actresses, cajoling them, flattering their sometimes dubious talents, all to achieve his own ends. She would definitely have to be on her guard: those Prussian blue eyes that twinkled with devilish lights were deceptive. He was a very perceptive man and he saw deeply. She could fully understand how easily women fell in love with him, each one no doubt thinking she was special. He certainly could be very charming; but Jenny convinced herself that she was immune.

A cold gust of winter wind blew against them once they had left the warmth of the centrally heated studio building, shattering Jenny's thoughts as she wrapped her coat about her. It tossed her flaxen hair into immediate disorder, blowing it into a halo around her face. It whipped against her tender face and she struggled to smooth it away.

Thaddeus leaned forward, brushing the thick shimmering strands from her face. The gesture was innocent enough, casual, yet it seemed strangely intimate. She could almost feel her skin warming because of his touch, and a spark deep within her began to flare.

As their eyes locked, Jenny was surprised by the way Thaddeus's gentle touch created such a response in her. All he had done was to carefully brush away her windblown hair. A harmless enough gesture, so why had it left her feeling so shaken? Jenny had submerged her feelings well during the last two years, hiding them even from herself. It must merely be the jolt of seeing Pablo again, and the prospect of working with him, that had forced this strange reaction . . .

CHAPTER TWO

IT WAS a short walk to the club. It was not officially part of the company, but the film company staff seemed to use it to the extent that calls often came from the studios to the bar.

'I'll just have a sandwich—chicken—and a coffee, no sugar,' Jenny informed him as she slipped into one of the booths. Her appetite was still not back to normal, and she ate lightly, so tried to keep her diet high in protein. She was still quite slim, but her curves were filling out and she was enjoying her new body image.

She glanced around; it was full as usual, even at this hour. She watched Thaddeus make his way to the bar. His tall, muscular body weaved effortlessly despite his size through the jostling crowd. They all stepped back as he approached, smiling at him, calls of friendship beckoning him to have a drink with them. He acknowledged them all with a wave, refusing their offers as he began to make his order.

Jenny felt a stab of annoyance at his obvious popularity, yet it was impossible to deny: despite his abrupt, almost rude manner he did appear to be well liked. He returned within moments, passing her a plate of hot food—saffron rice with a spicy hot chilli.

'Do you want some garlic bread?' he offered, the dark mop of his unruly hair falling across his face. He tossed it back casually, smiling at Jenny, deliberately refusing to acknowledge the look of wrath on her face.

24

'I asked for chicken,' she informed him coldly. The memories of how people had forced her to eat still rankled, and she felt a spiral of fury twist through her body. Still, that was all in the past now; she had overcome her difficulty, and she could even enjoy food. She tried to remain immune to the enticing aromas that were rising from her plate.

'I know,' he agreed, nodding between mouthfuls, 'but this is better. Now eat,' he commanded in a voice that warned her not to disagree.

Jenny was about to protest further, but the grim look on his face and the sternness in his eyes silenced any objections. She was feeling extremely hungry, she acknowledged silently. Although she hated to admit it, the food was excellent, ideal for a cold winter's day. She personally was grateful that the portions were so small, but she could well understand why most people took the salad and garlic bread that were offered with the meal.

'See,' said Thaddeus triumphantly, his eyes now gleaming with the light of supremacy as he viewed her empty plate, 'you were more hungry than you thought. I bet you never eat properly,' he said, looking at her critically, his expression darkening slightly. Jenny flushed, conscious that he had hit the nail right on the head, and she wondered how much he knew about her. He made a studied inventory of her body, slowly caressing every curve with unconcealed interest.

'I do,' she protested as he continued to study her with an intent she found strangely exciting. She enjoyed the effect her figure had on men; it was all so new, a novelty. Thaddeus leant back casually, but Jenny was not fooled by his posture and she eyed him warily. All her instincts were warning her about this man.

'Do you like the sun?' he asked, idly stroking the stem of his glass as he awaited her reply.

Jenny blinked, distracted by his abrupt change of conversation but grateful for it all the same. 'Sun—what do you mean?' she asked, puzzled, knowing there was more to the question and guarding herself.

'Sun, sea, sand, hot climates with cool drinks,' he teased, toying with his glass. But she was not taken in by his relaxed body. She shrugged.

'I suppose it's one type of holiday,' she admitted cautiously.

'But doesn't that type of climate really appeal in depths of a British winter?' he insisted, his bright blue eyes brimming with innocence and his mouth widening into a charming smile that could have melted the stoniest of hearts.

'Yes, I suppose so,' replied Jenny, confused, as she tried to keep her defence walls under the fire of his charm. 'Why do you ask?' There was a sudden flash of light in his eyes which could have been amusement or irritation, but whatever it was it had gone before she had a chance to detect its source.

'*The Devil's Captive*, the historical drama I'm going to do, is being filmed on location in Tunisia,' he informed her, thoroughly enjoying his teasing banter, a low rumble of laughter catching in his chest. The glee in his voice showed that she had fallen too easily into his trap.

Jenny felt her blood boil. She was astonished by the way he had managed to manipulate her. She drew a deep breath; he was too smooth for comfort, too clever by half and too charming by far. Jenny had been fooled once by such charisma, by the bright dazzle of a charming smile; but not this time, she vowed silently.

'I'm not going,' she replied stiffly, hiding the tumultuous emotions that were threatening to surface. She had only just, in the last few months, come to terms with what had happened, and she knew herself she was not ready to face Pablo yet.

Thaddeus lifted a dark brow and gave her a slow grin which seemed to contain light and warmed her very soul. Jenny couldn't help but respond; she lowered her eyes to avoid his penetrating gaze. She tried in vain to suppress the unexpected shiver his touch generated as his long fingers wrapped around her hand.

'Am I really that bad?' he asked, a tenderness in his voice she had not expected. Jenny shook her head.

'I've other arrangements, that's all,' she lied, not wishing to discuss her private life with him. Yet the look of concern on his face almost persuaded her to tell him the truth. His eyes pinned her, cutting through the barrier that she had erected as a protective shield, his already handsome face lit with a sensuous smile. He laid her soul bare, the intensity of his stare was so strong.

Jenny swallowed the lump that was growing by the second in her throat.

'Can't you cancel them?' His voice was coaxing, almost pleading in tone. He sat opposite her, leaning closer. Their legs touched momentarily and Jenny quickly withdrew them, tucking them as far as she could under her chair. He smiled, aware of what she had done, but Jenny didn't care. If he wanted to imagine that it was due to some attraction on her part he was very much mistaken.

Yet the physical presence of the man was hard to deny. He had an unspoken aura about him that pervaded his every move. There was an agility in his movements that aroused feelings in Jenny she'd thought she no longer possessed.

She kept control by breathing deeply, and sipped her black coffee so that he was forced to release her hand. Jenny knew he was awaiting a reply, and she unconsciously licked her mouth, giving her lips a gloss that enhanced their fullness.

'I have other arrangements and I'm not prepared to cancel them. There are dozens of others who would be delighted to go.' Jenny's voice was chillingly formal; there was no trace of the turmoil of emotions that were raging within her. Thaddeus frowned, and raked his hair from his face in a gesture of increasing frustration.

'I need you.' His voice was controlled, but his anger was evident by the tightening of the muscle in his face, making him look dangerous. His chiselled features seemed to grow even harder and a shiver of alarm raced through Jenny's body.

'Why?' asked Jenny; she was good at her job, but not to the extent that she was irreplaceable!

'I just think it would be good, that's all; we work well together.' His voice had a hollow ring and Jenny had seen no evidence that they worked well together. She viewed him with distrust, alarm bells ringing furiously in her brain as she struggled to think of a possible reason for his insistence.

'I'll think about it,' she answered untruthfully as she put her cup down, forcing herself to remain calm.

His features flashed with barely restrained frustration. 'Why is it I get the distinct impression you don't really mean that?' he asked, leaning across the table till he was close enough for her to feel his breath on her face. The sensation had the impact of a physical caress and Jenny's mouth went dry.

'I'm considering it.'

Thaddeus nodded knowingly, his strong fingers massaging the bottom of his chin as he viewed her with interest. 'You realise, of course, that I could request your services through official channels and you would be forced to come then.'

'No doubt you could,' Jenny admitted quietly, not trusting herself to look at him. His close proximity had sent her heart pounding.

'I prefer persuasion, though, don't you, Jennifer?' His deep voice did something wonderful to her name, giving it an intimacy that made her feel as if she was hearing it for the first time. Jenny said nothing. Instead she reminded herself that to Thaddeus this was no more than a well-planned game designed to make her go with him. She had seen him in action too many times: flattery, charm, romantic persuasion were all his tactics. He rarely had to resort to pulling rank.

'I'm not promising anything,' she reminded him as she stood to leave. He took a long visual tour of her body, giving Jenny the impression that he could see right through the material to her naked skin.

'Perhaps I'll be able to change your mind,' he said.

Jenny pulled her coat tighter around her slim body as he stood to face her.

'Don't hold your breath,' she warned him, determined to remain impervious to his charm.

He chuckled, seeing her defiance as amusing, which irritated Jenny all the more. He leaned over and straightened the collar of her coat. The touch of his warm hand on the nape of her neck made her quiver again with excitement. His touch was so gentle, yet still retained a strong masterfulness.

She looked up at his powerfully handsome face. She could feel the electric sensations that raced through her body. His pungent aftershave seemed to fill her nostrils and without being aware of it she had moved closer to him. It was essential she be on this location, her whole job depended on her being there, and he was hell-bent on making her go.

'The set is ready for this afternoon, isn't it?' he asked crisply as he swung open the club door, the familiar ring of authority back in his voice. Jenny felt herself stiffen with anger. He certainly wasted no time with polite chit-chat.

'Everything is ready,' she retorted abruptly as she swept past him.

'I hope so. I have enough catching up to do,' he rejoined with a trace of annoyance in his voice.

'I can assure you everything has been completed—unless of course you have changed your mind and not informed me again,' she reminded him. She was proficient at her job, and as the workload had increased she had tried even harder to keep pace. The threat of redundancy was ever-present these days.

Outside, the icy wind was still blowing fiercely and sleet was falling, making the path slippery and dangerous. The sky was leaden and the threat of a snowfall was evident. Jenny shivered, but as another frosty blast forced her back she felt the strong arms of Thaddeus wrap immediately around her. She tried to move, but his grip tightened as he held her close to him.

She stiffened, her spine erect. The whole length of her back was resting on the warm firmness of Thaddeus's body, and the impact was overwhelming. He bent his head, his smoky voice caressing her ear.

'Doesn't the thought of hot sunshine and miles upon miles of white beaches appeal?' he coaxed seductively, rocking her gently as he spoke.

Jenny swallowed, her mind racing. 'Yes,' she acknowledged carefully as the wind whipped relentlessly at her face, stinging her with its ferocity. Thaddeus released her slowly, but linked his arm through hers, a smile of victory on his face. Jenny protested, afraid of being seen: the film industry seemed to be made up of gossips, who would read so much into the most innocent of situations. Thaddeus remained undeterred.

'Let them talk. There's bound to be plenty now you've agreed to come to the filming of the next drama with me,' he teased, his easy tone matching the slumbrous invitation in his eyes.

Jenny came to an abrupt halt, her body shaking more with fury than cold.

'I agreed that this type of weather makes one think of warmer climates, but that does *not* mean I'm coming with you to Tunisia,' she declared, sounding as frozen as the wind that was sweeping around them.

'I'm sure you will, though,' he said, his arrogance infuriating her, but she decided she would have the good grace not to show it. She gave her slim shoulders a slight shrug of indifference, though she already was feeling confused.

'What is it with you and Margaret Miller?' he asked, putting his hand around her shoulder as they battled against the wind down the busy street. Jenny trembled at his touch. Was it desire, she wondered, from his physical touch, or had he probed a raw nerve mentioning Margaret Miller? He knew there was something preventing her from accepting the job offer, and it certainly wasn't just him. It was a shot in the dark, but he knew it had hit the bull's-eye when she stiffened and the colour drained from her face. She looked away, far away into the distance, her eyes staring and unseeing.

'Jennifer?'

She had grown even colder, her face ashen.

'She's an excellent actress,' she whispered through thinly parted lips. Their footsteps had grown slower and they were barely making any progress.

'True,' agreed Thaddeus, his face suddenly serious and thoughtful. He pushed her gently into an empty coffee-shop and steered her towards a table. His grip had tightened around her shoulder, but she seemed oblivious to his actions. He studied her countenance carefully. She looked so fragile, like a child, her paleness emphasising the brightness in her hazel eyes. He sat opposite her waiting for her to reply but she remained silent, unable to speak, as her mind raced with bitter memories.

'Margaret Miller?' he asked again, gently probing. He stroked his full bottom lip thoughtfully with his thumb and watched her reaction. Jenny sensed that he didn't want to hurt her—he was just curious about the true reason for her behaviour.

'I think she is one of the best,' Jenny admitted with difficulty; her mouth was dry and tears threatened to fall. In a way she longed to see Margaret again, but she couldn't now, not with Pablo there. It would be impossible.

'Granted, but that wasn't what I asked you, Jennifer. And I certainly don't believe that the fact that Margaret Miller is a brilliant actress is what's making your heart beat so wildly.'

She drew back, all too aware how helpless she must appear at this very moment. Thaddeus stared at her, realising far too much. It was impossible to lie to the man. She could try, but she felt instinctively that he would see right through her. Her deep pain was reflected, and for an instant she saw a flash of recognition in his eyes. Was it pity he was feeling? she wondered, but the effect was too quick and she was unable to be sure. This was her private grief, too deep to be shared, though she knew that he was determined not to be put off, and to find out the truth.

'I'm sorry, it isn't really any of my business,' he said, trying to put the subject to one side but obviously mentally vowing to find out. 'Coffee,' he barked, flashing a glare of wrath at the poor waitress who darted between them, and bringing Jenny back to the present.

'There isn't that much to tell, so you needn't dig about trying to find out,' she said suddenly as she caught the puzzled look on his face. She knew he would carry on wanting to know so decided on a half-truth; she would give him some of the story, not all—enough to satisfy him. She couldn't stand the risk of anyone knowing the whole truth.

'You don't have to tell,' he said gruffly, leaning back as the waitress deposited two steaming cups of coffee in front of them. Jenny eyed him warily over the rim of her cup.

'There's no great mystery; it's all in the past and best forgotten, that's all,' she explained. She took a sip of her coffee and grimaced; it was white and sweet. 'I had a silly girlish crush on a boy called Paul Hopwood. He dropped me for someone else—that's it.'

Thaddeus stared hard at her, awaiting more, but she was enjoying watching him trying not to ask questions when his mind was racing.

'Paul Hopwood is better known to you as Pablo Tagore.'

She knew the impact those words would make, and she had not underestimated his response. His eyebrows rose in disbelief and he gave a low whistle.

'You certainly do move in high places,' he said coolly. 'He's known worldwide for his acting ability.'

Jenny gave a grim smile by way of reply. Paul had certainly fooled her by his acting ability, she thought bitterly.

'He wasn't that famous when I knew him,' she admitted with an edge to her voice.

'So that's why you don't want to come and work with him?' Thaddeus queried, a expression of disbelief furrowing his brow.

'Not entirely. I would just prefer not to see him again, and I *am* tired. I could do with just getting away from it all.'

She hoped she sounded convincing; she was tired—exhausted really.

'It must have hurt you a great deal for you to still feel bitter,' he observed coolly. Jenny winced inside at his perceptiveness and felt herself colour.

'It was painful at the time but I'm over it now,' she retorted, her voice raising in self-defence. The mocking look on Thaddeus's face confirmed what she already knew: he didn't believe her.

'It was a long time ago. I was very young,' she admitted, still guarding how much she would say.

He fixed her with cold scrutiny, sending a shiver of anticipation down her spine. She knew she was gabbling. Who was she trying to convince—herself or Thaddeus? Jenny prayed desperately that he had accepted her story.

She tilted her head back to look at him, her expression serious. 'You understand I wouldn't want this to be widely known? Too many questions would be asked,' she explained.

Thaddeus swept over her uplifted face in a slow perusal which gave Jenny the impression he was choosing his next words very carefully. Then he shook his head.

'Thaddeus?'

He seemed to hesitate; she had revealed as much of her soul as she could bear; never before had she told anyone—surely he realised that?

'By the way, Margaret Miller mentioned you. Why would she do that?' he asked casually, as if changing the subject. Jenny drew a deep breath and her hands knotted nervously on the table-top. She wouldn't tell him. She had been used before because of her connection with Margaret Miller, and she vowed she would never let that happen again.

'I really don't know—you would have to ask her.' She tried to make her voice sound light and indifferent, but there was an unmistakable tremor in it.

'I might just do that,' he replied, and even if he didn't mean it Jenny felt very threatened. Her head shot up, fear rocketing through her. She wanted to slap him hard to wipe the smug, satisfied expression from his face, to scream at him that it was not of his business. Instead she took a deep breath. Patience has its own reward, she reminded herself.

Her fingers gripped the cup again as she tossed her head back and swallowed, wishing it contained something stronger than milky coffee.

Thaddeus was watching hard. She was always so polite, so in control, no matter what the provocation—yet he could see the battle now raging within her.

'You could always make sure I didn't by coming on location with me,' he murmured, triumph curling his lips. Jenny's expression gave away nothing. It was smooth, polite—even distant. But there was a dark storm brewing in her mind. She remained silent, knowing that her lack of response frustrated him.

'I wonder what worries you most—Pablo Tagore or me?' His voice was now warm and seductive and he moved dangerously close again.

Jenny was on her feet within seconds, flashes of amber colouring her eyes with a fire he had not expected.

'God, but you're arrogant! Tell me, Mr Clarke, why is it so important to you that I come on this job?' She was shouting, she knew she was, but he had pushed her too far. His insistence on her being on this shoot was bordering on the ridiculous. He ran a finger lightly across her hand and she felt her skin ripple with delight; it was exciting and frightening.

'Calm down, I was joking.' He sounded controlled and gentle. Jenny felt herself sink back down, her emotions still in turmoil. 'Perhaps you're right—perhaps I would find you too much of a distraction.' Then words deserted her as his hand reached out and slowly traced down the side of her face. She shuddered, her senses telling her to pull back, yet her traitorous body seeming to move slowly towards him.

He lifted her hand to his soft lips, then, with a gesture that turned her to liquid, he lifted each tingling fingertip to his mouth and kissed them slowly, one at a time, before pressing a firm, provocative kiss against the tender skin of her palm.

Jenny's heart soared, her blood racing through her veins with delight. Releasing her hand, Thaddeus cupped his long fingers under her chin. Without needing to use any force, he drew her towards him with a light, enticing pull that caused her to respond despite the protestions within her mind. She gave a low gasp at the initial contact; she wasn't prepared for the total explosion of feeling that erupted through her, giving life to every nerve as her mouth met his. When she tried to tug herself away, Thaddeus shook his head.

'No,' he said, 'not yet.'

His eyes were as liquid and as blue as the sea. He looked deep into her own eyes and, seeing no resistance, Thaddeus returned his mouth to hers. As he kissed her wonderfully, lingeringly, Jenny found herself wrapped in a warm cocoon of sensual pleasure. She moaned softly as his tongue traced a ring of flames around the edge of her softly parted lips. Her skin grew hot as she returned his kisses with a passion she had not thought possible. She ran her fingers through his dark hair, enjoying the rippling sensation and the way the ebony strands curled between them. It seemed an eternity before they drew apart and Thaddeus released her. He coolly drank in her flushed softened features.

'I knew it.'

'Knew what?'

'I knew the real reason for your not coming,' he mocked. 'Despite your frigid attitude to me I knew instinctively how you felt,' he gloated. Jenny knew it would be useless to deny his words, after what they had just shared, but all the same she certainly wasn't going to give him the satisfaction of believing he was irresistible.

'If this means an end to your insistence that I work with you, then it's a small price to pay,' she said coolly, viewing him with distaste.

Thaddeus framed her stern face with his palms. 'I'll take the kiss as deposit,' he taunted. 'Now, where does that leave us?'

'Nowhere,' she insisted. 'I've already told you. I've no intention of going to North Africa with you.'

'You can never be that sure in life.'

Jenny shook her head. The man simply refused to listen. 'Are you always this stubborn?'

'Always. I never give up.' His eyes sparkled with unrepressed humour. 'Jennifer?'

'What is it now?' she snapped, irritated by the way he seemed to consider her feelings and objections as tiresome obstacles, easily overcome. Thaddeus ran a finger down her cheek, causing a fresh flurry of emotions to stir deep within her. Jenny's lips curled in automatic response.

'Think about it?' he asked coaxingly.

Jenny stared at him, unable to answer, still reeling from his kiss; she could find no excuse for her reaction. She now was more determined than ever to steer a wide berth between her and Thaddeus. She would not allow herself to become the next poor victim of his devilish charm. He seemed to imagine it was a perk of the job to seduce any female he wanted. The trail of brokenhearted girls who still longed for his company never ceased to amaze Jenny, but anyway, she was too wary of men and too professional to get involved with a colleague.

'I think we'd better get back to work,' she replied, making her way to the door. 'Thanks for lunch and the coffee,' she added, though she wasn't sure whether she owed him thanks or not.

They had only gone a few steps when a cheery voice rang out behind them.

'Hey, Thad, hold up—I'll walk back with you. Still on *Private Lies*?' asked Michael O'Shea, the lighting director, as he joined them. Jenny was grateful for the intrusion, as it meant she could leave and not be subjected to a further cross-examination from Thaddeus.

Jenny was delighted when, later that afternoon, the missing actors returned, complaining loudly to Thaddeus in good-humoured banter.

Filming resumed, and Thaddeus once again became the perfectionist, demanding the highest standards from everyone. Jenny worked hard, replacing the correct details in the schedules and ensuring that everyone knew exactly when they were needed. She was walking back to the canteen with a tray of coffees when Jill from Personnel stopped her.

'What new dates are you changing your holidays to?' she asked a puzzled Jenny.

'Pardon?'

'Holiday—I thought you were taking a fortnight off starting Friday week?' she said curiously.

'I am—that leave has been in for months,' Jenny assured her as a wave of worry crossed her thoughts. Jill shook her head and gave a wry laugh.

'But they've been cancelled,' she explained to a stunned Jenny.

'Cancelled—by whom?' Jenny demanded angrily at Jill's words, her mind already having its suspicions.

'No idea. I just noticed that the roster has been changed; Peggy has taken yours and you're down to go...'

'To Tunisia,' Jenny offered.

'That's right—aren't you lucky? I wish I could go.' Jill began to prattle on as they continued down the corridor, but Jenny wasn't even listening; her mind was on one thing alone. Suddenly an idea struck her.

'Can I still have that fortnight if I want?' she asked.

'What on earth...? If I had the opportunity...'

'Jill,' snapped Jenny in order to silence her, 'could I still have those weeks?'

'Yes, of course—there are plenty of PAs this time of year, and anyone from an agency would jump at the chance to go to Tunisia. I know I would.'

'Yes, all right, but I really do not want to go. Re-book my holidays, and in no circumstances change them unless I ask you personally, OK?' Jenny informed her coolly, amazed at her own outward composure when she was seething inwardly with rage. Jill nodded and scurried off.

Jenny was so furious at Thaddeus's high-handed attitude that she totally ignored the flashing red light. She stormed on to the set, marching straight across the moving scene that was so carefully being acted out. There was a roar of protest by all concerned, then silence as Thaddeus strode out, his face as dark as a midnight sky.

'What on earth do you think you're doing?' he bellowed, his voice shattering the pregnant silence like the crack of a whip. He placed both his hands firmly on his hips, his legs apart as he waited for her to reply. There was silence on the set as everyone from stage-hands to actors watched the scene before them with unconcealed interest.

Jenny glared at him, unperturbed by his reaction—she was far too furious to care. They stood facing one another. He was like a raging bull, his nostrils flaring and his eyes shining with a glittering fire.

Jenny drew herself up to confront him.

'How dare you change my holidays? You have no right...' she began, her voice surprisingly steady despite the turmoil she felt inside. She was unable to finish the sentence, though, for Thaddeus had taken her wrist in an unshakeable grip and was hauling her out of the studio. Jenny's protestations fell on deaf ears and she stumbled as he virtually dragged her out of the room.

Once outside, he flung her unceremoniously on to a chair and stood in front of her, freezing her to the spot with a glacial look.

'I have been setting up that scene for the last two hours. Finally it was beginning to come together and you ruined it.' He spoke quietly, emphasising each word with chilling menace. Jenny stared at the throbbing vein in his temple, fascinated and frightened at the same time. She had learned to cope with his outrageous outbursts, his noisy tirades that shook the set with their ear-shattering loudness. Now she realised it was all an act, a pretence at anger to ensure results. Here was the man when he was truly furious, and fear ran the length of Jenny's spine. Suddenly he seemed so much larger than usual, tall and intimidating. His body was like steel, hard and inflexible; his features had grown more forbidding, and Jenny felt herself shrink back. The look of unleashed violence was evident in that throbbing beat of his brow and the tightness of his hard jaw, and she watched him warily as he drew closer, the freezing contempt mirrored in his eyes. Unconsciously her hands curled into tight fists, ready to fight him off, if need be.

She swallowed and took a deep breath before answering him; she could see the dark storm threatening. 'You had no right to change my holiday.' She tried to make her voice sound controlled, but there was an undeniable tremor present.

'Tough,' he snapped back, his expression hardening at her obvious defiance. Jenny jumped to her feet, heedless to the fact that her pulses were as frantic as a bee's wings.

'You chauvinistic pig,' she spat at him in fury. 'Do you honestly think you have the right to do that?'

Self-satisfaction seemed to ooze from his every pore as his lips curled into a mocking smile.

'I've done it,' he answered her smoothly. He watched her thoughtfully, looking at the sparks emanating from her and her tiny fists so tense and angry. Jenny, too steeped in her own exasperation, failed to notice his appreciative study.

'Well, I've changed them back,' she retorted. Damn. She sounded like a petulant child, and he responded to her as if she were.

'I see,' he said gravely, his voice low and calm, but she could hear the intensity shrouded just beneath the surface, still bubbling away, waiting to erupt.

'I've told you—I need that holiday.' There was a plea in her voice that he could not help but respond to. His sombre gaze plumbed the soft hazel depths of her eyes, seeing the unspoken fear. He knew instinctively that she was not being honest; there was more to it than her need for a holiday.

'Is that the only reason?' he asked, his voice rough. She didn't answer for a moment, and when she raised her head her eyes were soft with unshed tears.

'Yes,' she said quietly, lifting her shoulders in a half-shrug. She was lying and she knew Thaddeus wanted to know the truth.

'OK, let's just forget it for the moment,' he suggested, and gratitude flooded into Jenny's eyes; but she knew that Thaddeus was resolute in his decision to have Margaret Miller play the leading role—and if that meant taking his troublesome PA with him, then she would have to go, regardless of how she felt.

CHAPTER THREE

JENNY looked carefully at her reflection. She wanted to look perfect tonight. At last the filming was completed, and tonight was the end-of-shoot party. This was a customary party paid for by the company and everyone who was involved in the production usually attended. It was a chance for final farewells and good-luck wishes.

Jenny was determined not to stay too long; she still had to drive to Apinold, the tiny village where she had recently bought herself a small two-bedroomed cottage. It was an ideal location, rural enough to be a cosy retreat yet within an hour's drive of the city.

She hoped tonight to secure her position, which might have been jeopardised by her refusal to go to Tunisia. She wanted to look efficient despite the party atmosphere. She looked in the mirror again, delighted at her reflection. It was not that many years ago that she'd been a plump, shapeless teenager, full of silly schoolgirl dreams. She gave a rueful smile; she certainly had changed from an ugly duckling into a beautiful swan.

It was important for Jenny to be seen as beautiful—it gave her confidence a boost; but rarely did she have the opportunity to dress up. Tonight she had pulled her usual unruly tresses into a sophisticated French plait that fastened at the nape of her neck with a large black bow trimmed with a row of pearl buttons. She had barely applied any make-up; with her peach-coloured complexion it was hardly necessary. She used only a delicate

damask rose blusher and a matching lip-gloss. Her hazel
eyes were enhanced by a soft brown eye-shadow, barely
visible, and framed by naturally long lashes, giving them
a striking appeal. She wore a black silk suit which had
a double row of buttons down the front and she softened
its austerity with a string of pearls around her neck and
matching studs at her ears. Jenny stared in disbelief at
her reflection and turned slowly in front of the mirror
to ensure everything was perfect.

When she entered the bar she was innocently unaware
of the impact she made. She walked in, her head held
high, her eyes dancing with anticipation, a gentle smile
of welcome on her soft lips. There was a buzz of conversation at her transformation; even the dark suit could
not hide the shapely curve of her body, yet most days
Jenny wore baggy tracksuits, as she found them so
comfortable, especially when on location.

She idly picked up a glass of white wine and sipped
it appreciatively as she surveyed the hall. Her eyes travelled quickly around the room. She recognised everyone
and gave them a gentle smile of acknowledgement. She
then slipped into an alcove seat; she didn't want to join
a group as she knew then the chances of an early getaway
would be impossible.

She leant back, closing her eyes and sighing quietly
to herself. She enjoyed her job, it was interesting and
challenging, but she longed for the peace of her rural
retreat. The stark contrasts in her lifestyle complemented one another, but Jenny's real heart was in the
solitude of her country home. She enjoyed the excitement of the film world, it was part of her, yet she
had never been truly happy with it.

She picked up her glass and took a large mouthful of her wine, hoping it would act as a tranquilliser as bitter memories threatened to surface. It was hard to rid oneself of the past, but Jenny had grown strong over the past couple of years, and she was growing more confident every day.

She stiffened as she noticed that Thaddeus had entered. He certainly shook her equilibrium, despite her attempts to remain immune to him. Even at a distance Thaddeus managed to exude strength and masculinity. Tonight he looked even more dangerous, panther-like in his dark suit, his body lean and hard. His hair was gleaming like a raven's wing under the coloured lights.

Jenny watched him with quiet fascination. He had not mentioned the Tunisia job to her since their row, but she felt he was merely waiting for the opportunity. The last week of filming had gone extremely smoothly, and an uneasy truce had been forged between them. Jenny had made sure she kept her distance from him. She still did not trust him: there was something threatening in the way he looked at her.

Despite all her mental abilities that warned her to beware, however, her body seemed intent on betrayal. The mere sound of his voice seemed to generate a *frisson* of delight within her. She watched him disappear into the crowd and settled back with relief. She tried to regain her composure, closing her eyes to allow the music to soothe her troubled mind. Slowly she began to drift into a dreamy state.

'Miss Collins.' It was Peggy Grant, the head of Personnel and Jill's boss. Her voice was sharp and it had a cutting edge. Jenny remained silent, her mind in turmoil, her heart racing. She hadn't expected this, yet

Thaddeus's smug expression as he stood with the older woman was confirmation of her worst fears. 'Mr Clarke and I have been discussing the possibility of your changing your plans so that you can accompany the film crew out to Tunisia.' She smiled, but without warmth. Jenny returned the smile and at the same time couldn't help but notice the possessive grip Peggy had on Thaddeus's arm. Jenny could feel Thaddeus's cool appraisal of her. His gaze travelled over her body, taking in every curvaceous outline with unconcealed interest. He didn't appear to miss an inch.

A tingling sensation had immediately spread throughout Jenny's body. There was a tangible aura between them both that was impossible to deny. Jenny stared into the hypnotic blue depths of Thaddeus's eyes and was treated to one of his most charming smiles. A huge grin spread across his handsome face, revealing his perfect white teeth. She noted his broad shoulders and wide chest; his stomach was flat and his narrow hips and strong, muscular thighs fitted snugly against his smooth black trousers. It was almost impossible to deny such an attractive man anything he asked for.

'Well, Jennifer, if there's any chance?' His voice was warm and friendly, yet somehow there was a ring of challenge about it that only Jenny seemed to pick up.

'I feel quite sure, Mr Clarke, that you know my feelings on this subject,' replied Jenny, hardly conscious of uttering a sound, though somehow the words emerged despite herself. The knot in her stomach tightened as he took a step closer. She felt him take her hand, his grip was firm and warm. Her body trembled inwardly at his touch and she hoped the impact he was making was not visible.

'Let's talk about it as we dance,' he coaxed gently as he pulled her softly to her feet. The sound of his voice caressed her ear and the warmth of his proximity sent shivers down her spine. She was going to object, but the green-eyed look of jealousy on Peggy's face encouraged her to join him.

Jenny weakened as she caught the pungent smell of his aftershave when he pulled her effortlessly towards him. She felt troubled by the intensity of emotion he seemed to arouse in her with so little effort. It had been so long since she had felt this alive.

She closed her eyes as the painful memories came flooding back. A haunting dark image of Pablo flashed across her mind with nightmarish realism, the hurt seeping into her bones like an unhealthy virus soon to be replaced by anger. It began to bubble up inside her like a pot on the stove. Jenny struggled to remain in control, but Thaddeus was awakening in her feelings she was determined never to acknowledge again. Damn him! she silently cursed as she tried to smile sweetly.

'You're obviously not aware how important this job is, Jennifer,' he explained. 'Most people would be willing to change their holiday dates. There will be a great deal of prestige to this job,' he stated arrogantly.

Jenny paused, her body suddenly stiff. There was an edge to her voice that did not go unnoticed. 'I'm afraid prestige doesn't interest me as much as it concerns you.'

He glanced over her smoothly. Any softness in his eyes had disappeared, his manner changed.

'Miss Collins, I find your reluctance even to consider the job slightly tiresome, and I should like the real reason for your dissent,' he retorted, very much in command.

Jenny struggled inwardly, swallowing her temper, though her fingers itched to slap his hard, handsome face. She carefully managed to retain her aloofness, though her contempt was clearly visible. 'Mr Clarke, my reasons for not wanting to go are personal,' she replied in a clipped tone. She turned abruptly to go, but a strong grip around her tiny waist prevented her.

Thaddeus's eyes narrowed, hard and dangerous, rendering Jenny speechless. 'I've got to have you there,' he said in a hoarse whisper. His voice had a threatening edge, and Jenny found the tall unleashed strength of his body daunting. His quiet tone was more of a menace than his usual noisy outbursts. She could feel his puzzlement giving rise to 'anger and outrage. His face darkened as they surveyed one another.

Jenny looked into Thaddeus's eyes, searching deep into his soul. She was trying to fathom a reason for his insistence, but found none. There was a disturbing sensation radiating between them. He stood entirely still, not uttering a word; the music seemed to be mocking their lack of movement as the beat increased around them. Jenny was unable to answer him. No one must ever know the whole truth, she thought desperately, her heart beating furiously against her chest. She knew he was waiting for an explanation and he certainly did not believe her need for a holiday.

'I'm going into hospital next week for a minor operation,' she said coolly at last, amazed that she had not thought of this simple white lie before. The look of puzzlement faded slowly from Thaddeus's face, to be replaced by his usual sophisticated composure. Then a wicked grin slowly crept over his face.

'I see, and as it *is* only minor it could wait till our return, yes?'

Jenny raised her eyes slowly, the long, sooty lashes that framed her hazel eyes curled upwards, gazing with total innocence into Thaddeus's eyes.

Her look sent a thrilling sensation through his body. How could an innocent arouse so strong a physical desire? he mused, as he looked down on her fresh youthful mouth.

Jenny was not about to weaken; this arrogant man would try any tactics, including charm, to get what he wanted. She shrugged her shoulders in a lazy manner, conveying in that one gesture the total disregard she had for his idea.

'I'm sorry, but no. I really must go into hospital,' she explained, strangely elated when he nodded in acceptance, though he still did not release her.

'OK. Let's dance,' he said curtly, his frown deepening as his mind raced, searching for a possible solution to his dilemma. Jenny faltered for a moment before gently picking up the rhythm of the music.

He drew her closer with expert skill. Jenny could feel his hard chest pressed up against her soft breasts and a thrill of excitement ran through her slender frame. He lifted her chin and held her face still, his eyes boring into hers with a depth that frightened her.

'I hope there's nothing seriously wrong?' he asked, his tone suggesting his disbelief of her statement.

'Please let me go,' Jenny almost pleaded, trying to keep a strength in her voice she knew she didn't personally possess. His touch was so unnerving, and he seemed to be touching her deliberately.

'Relax,' he told her, pulling her even closer. 'I only want to dance, talk a little.'

Jenny lowered her head in defeat. There was no point in struggling; it would only draw attention to them. She didn't want that—it was bound to start the gossip.

She swallowed deeply, taking a deep breath as she began to flow to the music. It was a modern enough sound, but the band was playing it in a waltz tempo— slow and seductive. Jenny felt helpless as he whirled her round softly, with considerable skill. At each turn he drew her nearer to him and she held herself tautly in defence as she began to feel her body surrendering to the aching need within her. She was too conscious of him, the smell of his woody aftershave, the texture of his skin, smooth and olive-toned. She was aware of the increasing pressure of his hard body against hers. Her pulses leapt as she was forced to accept the desire he was arousing in her. He slowly began to trace the outline of her lips, caressing them softly with his expert touch. Jenny gasped in surprise as she felt the sudden swell of passion.

'Stop it!' she pleaded, trying to move away, but her limbs had turned to jelly.

'Stop what?' he mocked, his sensuous mouth curling into a provocative smile. Jenny struggled against her own primitive appetite, replacing it with anger. She pushed her hands forcibly on his chest and for a moment thought she had succeeded in gaining her freedom; her palms stung as he remained unmoved. His masculine strength, though, was too much for her, and his arms were soon back round her body again.

'You seem to have taken a sudden dislike to dancing, and I thought we were doing so well,' he drawled.

'Dancing I like—it's my partner I have the distaste for,' retorted Jenny sharply, trying to edge away as she spoke.

'Really? And there are other women who would love to be dancing with me,' he said, smiling, ignoring her retort.

'Really? Then I suggest you ask them, because I've no——' began Jenny, but her words froze in the air as he pulled her even closer to him. Their bodies fused instantly as one. Jenny suddenly felt weak and oddly vulnerable. Then a wave of anger swept over her. How dared he treat her like this? she fumed inwardly, hating her own body's betrayal. She slowly raised her foot and in one movement stamped down hard on Thaddeus's feet, her temper giving it extra force. He withdrew his foot immediately and at the same time released her.

'Ouch—that hurt,' he complained, but there was a wry smile on his face.

'I'm so sorry—I must have two left feet,' apologised Jenny mockingly.

'Never mind—I'll teach you,' Thaddeus replied gently, taking her into his arms again. Jenny glared at him, her hazel eyes burning with sparks of golden fire.

'You have a high opinion of yourself. An expert dancer, are we now?' she snapped. It was then that the band stopped playing, and he released her gently but still kept a possessive grip on her hand. He steered her over to a quiet corner table.

'Do sit down, Jennifer,' he said gently, but his attitude gave little room for discussion. Jenny reluctantly slipped into a chair.

'If you would care to look at these shots,' said Thaddeus, pushing a large folder of colour photographs and slides over to Jenny, his eyes fastened on her, sparkling with devilish delight. 'There are a few shots of Tunisia that I think could be used, but I'd love you to do a recce with me next week,' he coaxed. Jenny stared at him in disbelief, and as a flush of pink coloured her face she stole a quick sideways glance.

'I've told you I'm not interested,' she said in a quiet whisper. Thaddeus shrugged his broad shoulders.

'I'm not saying agree to the job—it's merely that you want a holiday. Come to Tunisia, help me choose locations, and if you're still not convinced you can fly back by the end of the week. It will be like a holiday, all expenses paid.'

The offer was tempting; the white beaches seemed to beckon Jenny. She could almost feel the warmth of the sun on her face. She glanced down at the photographs. She had never been to Africa, and it certainly looked fascinating. Her eyes flicked towards his, a frown deepening on her forehead.

'Listen, Jennifer,' he began, the sound of her name on his lips sounding magical. He drew closer till he was next to her, his voice gentle and persuasive. 'I think you would be ideal for this trip.'

Jenny raised her eyebrows in disbelief and he noted her expression with amusement, his grin widening till it became infectious.

'Yes, I do,' he stated briskly before sighing as Jenny's expression grew more incredulous. 'OK, so we have had our disagreements, but you know your job and I know I can depend on you.' He paused for a moment while he ran his thumb thoughtfully across his sensuous mouth, and Jenny's eyes were trapped, watching his movement with quiet fascination. 'Well, most of the time,' he admitted. He sounded sincere, and then he smiled, his winning smile that could charm anyone, and Jenny felt herself weakening. She was secretly pleased he had such confidence in her, and yet she still had a niggling doubt. He was too machiavellian to pass a compliment without there being an ulterior motive. *Why* was he insisting on her going? she mused. It was all rather strange.

'I'm not sure,' she faltered, the strength in her voice holding more conviction than she felt. She loved to travel, and even at a glance she could tell that Tunisia would be beautiful.

'It will be an excellent opportunity—the story is marvellous,' he began, sensing that she was weakening. 'It's a project I've wanted to do for some time, ever since discovering the story,' he added mysteriously as he toyed with his glass and avoided the quizzical look on Jenny's face.

'Discovering the story—that's a bit dramatic, isn't it?' she cajoled him, sensing that he was deliberately trying to entice her.

The dimples in his cheeks deepened as he grinned in response. He leant closer and she caught the woody aroma of his aftershave, which was becoming dangerously familiar. His eyes were sparkling with a deep intensity she had not seen before. The glow in those dark blue depths sent a tingling sensation racing through her body.

'No,' he corrected her, amused that his ruse had been uncovered. He was confident he still held the trump card. 'I was holidaying in Spain, in a tiny hamlet miles from anywhere. The only place of interest was a run-down chapel and convent. It was high above in the hills, hardly accessible, but I had nothing better to do so I went visiting.' He paused while he sipped his drink, but Jenny was burning with curiosity—she knew there was more to his tale and was longing to hear it.

'Go on,' she whispered, her voice annoyingly husky as her body responded to him instinctively.

'It's a long story and it took me ages to piece together,' he said, half to himself. Jenny knew he was toying with her, dangling interesting snippets before her, enticing her till she took the bait. She looked at him thoughtfully, then nodded and smiled.

'I'm listening, Mr Clarke, and it had better be good!'

'It's better than good—it's terrific.' He laughed as he moved even closer and wrapped his strong arm across her shoulder in a conspiratorial manner. Jenny stiffened; her heartbeat immediately sped up and she could feel the warm glow rush to her cheeks. She hated blushing, but Thaddeus Clarke was all male, and he exuded a sexuality that demanded a response.

Without being conscious of her action Jenny relaxed and leant back on to his arm, ready to listen to the story. She caught the gleam of triumph in Thaddeus's eyes as he settled back, and after half an hour she knew the reason why. The story was truly fascinating.

A beautiful titled English lady was on her way to an arranged marriage when the ship was struck by pirates. She was taken for ransom but before long fell in love with her captor, a dashing, handsome man. He was known as the Devil because of his formidable reputation. She was finally, much to her consternation, released; however, she swore she was pregnant. The previously arranged marriage was naturally now annulled. Her desperate parents were forced to seek out the pirate captain. They obtained him a pardon and a title on the condition that he would marry their daughter and thereby avoid a scandal. He agreed, but unfortunately, the night before the wedding, the bride confessed to her maid that she was still a virgin. Her father, who overheard, was furious at the cunning deceit. In his anger, the father shot the husband-to-be at the foot of the altar. The devastated bride was so distraught that she entered a convent and was never heard of again.

'And is it a true story?' asked Jenny, breathless, her heart beating rapidly at such a tender, romantic tale.

'Yes, every detail—I've checked and double-checked,' he assured her confidently.

'I never had you down for a romantic person.' She smiled, her soft lips parting. Her eyes sparkled as she viewed him in a different light.

'Ah, well, there's lots you don't know about me,' his velvety voice teased. There was an invitation in those words, and Jenny studied him carefully. She felt drawn to him, it was pointless to deny it, but after Pablo she was cautious. She didn't trust Thaddeus Clarke—not an inch. He was too slick, too sure of himself, but despite all her misgivings the effect he had on her could not be denied. He aroused in her a sudden desire to change her sterile life to allow someone in again; but she was afraid the price she paid last time was too high. The memory robbed her cheeks of colour, and her eyes grew soft when she recalled how stupid she had been. She looked up quickly, aware that he was watching her, but his expression was unreadable. She sighed as she tried to figure out what to do. Had she grown enough to face Pablo, or would all the old pain resurface?

'It's a great story, don't you think?' Thaddeus asked, wanting to break the silence that was growing between them and knowing that her thoughts were not about the job.

'Yes, yes,' said Jenny, grateful that he had snapped her back from dwelling on the past. 'I think you're right; it will make a great film—perhaps even win a couple of awards,' she admitted almost reluctantly.

'Now, doesn't that make you want to come? Wouldn't you like to be part of a winning team?' Thaddeus's smoky voice said coaxingly as he allowed his arm to wrap around Jenny's shoulders. She gave a shiver at his touch and tried to move away. She looked into his face, but couldn't keep from her eyes the unwilling attraction she felt. There was a powerful aura between them as their eyes locked together, and Jenny lowered her head to avoid taking the full impact of his searing stare.

'Let's dance again; I want to talk.' It seemed more an order than a request, which infuriated Jenny. Her head shot upwards, her face spoilt by a frown.

'Last time was quite enough, thank you,' she retorted briskly.

'Last dance!' commanded Thaddeus, taking her arm and pulling her reluctantly to the floor. Once again she caught the pungent smell of his aftershave as he drew her close. She put her hand on his chest and could feel the strong beat of his heart thudding against her palm as she tried to push him away, but he was stronger and his arms wrapped even tighter around her. He pressed his body against hers, caressing her back with feather-light strokes that were melting her defences. He pressed a tormenting kiss on her forehead and Jenny's whole body became alive with desire. She was grateful for the darkness of the dance-floor; it made visibility difficult yet she felt quite sure he knew the effect he was having on her. A wry smile played on his lips as he moved his body rhythmically against hers, totally aware of the havoc he was causing. Jenny tried valiantly to hold herself tautly, though the seductive tempo of the music and the closeness of Thaddeus made it impossible.

'Why do you fight so strongly against such natural feelings?' he asked as he softly stroked the side of her face, a look of puzzlement on his face.

'The only desire I have at the moment is to go home to bed.' Jenny could have bitten her tongue the moment the words were spoken. She knew exactly what he would make of them and couldn't help but wonder herself whether it was a Freudian slip.

'I didn't mean like that...' she began, flustered. She could sense the mocking smile on his face, though she was unable to see it. He drew her closer, his lips brushing gently across hers, and she melted. Her flesh felt on fire, and she was burning inwardly. She knew he was about to kiss her but was too weak to pull away. He cradled her face, holding it captive, then his head swiftly descended on to her lips, capturing them before she had chance to escape. He stroked his hand through her hair and the natural waves wrapped themselves treacherously about his fingers. At first her response was stilted, but the series of gentle kisses made her weaken. The kiss caused her head to swim, a familiar flood of desire swept over her and she clung to him as she drowned in her own cravings. She struggled fruitlessly against the rising tide of emotion, fighting her rebellious body, which was softening instinctively at his low seductive voice.

'Beneath all that ice-cool composure, Jennifer, there is a very passionate woman,' his warm breath murmured, before their lips locked together again, the kiss hard and quick. 'What has made you bottle up your feelings?' he coaxed gently as he stroked her back with long, expert movements. Her body started to vibrate against him and Jenny pulled back, a series of alarm bells ringing violently in her head. She forced a shrug despite the rapid thudding of her heart.

'Excuse me a moment,' she said softly, her hands trembling gently as she pushed past him. Again she thought she saw a flicker of tenderness in his eyes, but it was quickly replaced by his usual poker expression. His eyes became uncharted depths, too dark for her to read.

Jenny fled to the ladies' room, her heart beating so rapidly that it was causing her pain. She turned the cold taps fully on and pushed her wrists underneath the pounding water. The fresh water soon numbed her hot hands and she felt her pulse decrease to a slow, steady rhythm. She dried her hands with care and retouched her make-up. She then sank wearily on to a chair as she tried to sort out her feelings towards Thaddeus Clarke. She felt she couldn't possibly go to Tunisia—the thought of seeing Pablo was too much—yet why should she miss the opportunity of travel and the chance of seeing Margaret again? Maybe the attraction she felt for Thaddeus could grow into something more.

She shivered at the thought. She had been down that path before; the attraction for Thaddeus would only last till someone else came along. She knew she wasn't prepared to be hurt like that again. But she could just go for the week, she argued inwardly with herself. It would be interesting as long as she kept Thaddeus at arm's length.

Jenny sighed, her mind finally made up, and strolled back to the table. She felt happier knowing her acceptance would not only please Thaddeus but enhance her career.

Thaddeus was too deep in conversation to notice that Jenny had returned, and his deep voice seemed to carry over the noise of the party.

'Yes, I think I've been successful; she will have thought about it and no doubt will agree.' His voice had an authority and assurance that infuriated her. She stopped dead in her tracks and listened, shocked, when she heard Sam reply,

'Well, the old charm never fails, eh? Women—they're suckers for it!'

The sound of Thaddeus's laughter echoed through Jenny's numbed body. She felt betrayed, and a searing pain cut into her soul. She had been such a fool; she should have known Thaddeus was only toying with her in order to make her agree. Jenny felt her face colour with humiliation, and without waiting to hear Thaddeus's reply she hurried from the room. She snatched her coat from the cloakroom and fled, suddenly longing to be in her own safe haven.

The drive home seemed longer than usual; although the cottage was quite remote, it still was ideal for commuting. The tiny village boasted a rail link and an excellent bus service to the city. Jenny hurried straight to bed without even bothering making herself a drink; she was far too tired and emotionally drained.

Next morning, Jenny blinked at the brightness that was filling her tiny room. Despite the heavy velvet curtains the white light seemed to pour in. She lay back and gazed at the cracked ceiling. The silence of the countryside was unusually quiet, almost eerie.

Reluctantly she slipped from her bed and drew back the heavy curtains. The snow that had been threatening for days had finally fallen, covering the countryside in a thick blanket of dazzling white snow. She shivered as she scanned the moorland. It looked beautiful, a picture postcard, but in this remote area it could mean untold problems. She was grateful that she had taken the precaution of stocking up her freezer; at least she wasn't in danger of starving. She grinned to herself. She hurried back into bed, curling up into a tight ball and hugging the duvet close to her chin for warmth and comfort, and gave a groan as the telephone began to ring. She had delayed putting one in for so long, but had been advised that in such a remote area it was essential. She frowned now, wishing she hadn't taken heed of that particular advice.

The caller was insistent and the ringing continued to shatter the comfortable silence. Jenny darted from the bed and scurried downstairs. Central heating as soon as I can afford it, she told herself as the cold morning air hit her. She picked up the phone, shivering as an icy draught swept under the door. She hopped from leg to leg, trying to generate some heat in her body.

'Hello?' she said, but no more—the second she heard that familiar voice she replaced the receiver with a bang. She allowed herself a smile of triumph as the phone began to ring immediately. She skipped back up the stairs and dived under the covers, laughing with childish joy as an image of Thaddeus's furious face flashed before her.

Throughout the day the telephone rang, and each time it was Thaddeus Jenny replaced the receiver without saying a word. Thankfully by late afternoon he had given up, and Jenny received no further calls. Finally she began to unwind. She had enjoyed her first day back at her cottage; she'd taken a short walk down to the local shop for some milk and had been warned that more bad weather was on the way. The danger of being snowed in quite appealed to Jenny. She had several books she wanted to catch up on, and she needed the rest, as the intensity of work the last few weeks had left her drained.

That evening she settled down after taking an early bath. She had made herself a thick, nourishing stew complete with dumplings, as her earlier walk had made her hungry and for once she wasn't going to think about weight-watching. She opened herself a bottle of rich red wine and placed it near the open fire to warm. Then she chose one of her favourite CDs and curled up in her armchair with a new novel. The music drifted sweetly around her and Jenny gave a smile of contentment as she looked around her room.

Suddenly there was a banging on her door. Jenny's heart leapt and she gave a cry of surprise. She jumped to her feet in fear. It couldn't possibly be a visitor; nobody would get through after this afternoon's further snowfall. Besides, everyone who knew her respected her privacy too much to just arrive unannounced.

She peered through the small pane of glass in the door, rubbing the condensation away as she tried to get a better picture of who it was. The shadow was certainly tall and ominous; she was just about to ask who it was when she was spotted.

'Open this bloody door, will you? I'm freezing,' Thaddeus's voice roared at her, his icy tone matching the chill in the night air. For a moment Jenny hesitated, but his voice came again, cracking like a whip across the desolation.

'For God's sake hurry up, before I die of exposure.'

Jenny knew it was no exaggeration; it could be deadly out there. The pass had closed shortly after her arrival—she remembered the radio giving out warnings. How on earth had he managed to get through? she thought as she flung open the door.

'How did you get here?' she asked as he stepped inside.

'I walked,' he snarled as he marched into the small lounge, his formidable large frame dwarfing the room still further. Jenny followed, feeling suddenly quite angry at his high-handed attitude. She was puzzled by his arrival and tried to give him a smile of welcome, but it soon died on her lips as she was confronted by the dark storm of anger that was swirling in the cold brilliance of his eyes.

CHAPTER FOUR

JENNY stared at him as he raised his hand and raked it through his thick dark hair. A flurry of snow cascaded down, and Jenny was tempted for a fleeting moment to make a joke about dandruff shampoos, but she somehow knew it would not be appreciated. Thaddeus cursed softly through his clenched white teeth as he strode over to the fire and began rubbing his hands in an attempt to get warm.

Jenny stared at him in disbelief. Her heart was beating furiously. She swallowed nervously and was amazed, when she spoke, at the calm control in her voice.

'What brings you here, Mr Clarke?' she asked as she watched him warm himself by her fire, effectively blocking the heat from the rest of the room by his strong physique.

She noticed that the thick layer of snow that clung to his scuffed boots was beginning to melt and seep into her carpet. There were also damp patches on his jeans, which seemed to cling with an intimate snugness to his body.

He straightened up to face her, his eyes darkening as he scanned her face with contempt. She was pleased that the room was only lit by a small table-lamp. The darkness acted as a shield; otherwise he would have seen her embarrassment at his cold scrutiny.

'You, of course,' he snarled, dragging his heavy-duty coat from his back and flinging it across a chair. There was a squeal of protest and Theo, the cat, darted from the room. Jenny's eyes followed Theo's departure with a frown, and her head snapped back to Thaddeus.

'I didn't see it,' he bit out, unable to stand the accusation in her eyes.

Jenny remained unmoved by his plea and viewed him silently.

'I didn't even know you had a cat,' he continued, almost apologetically.

Jenny continued to stare at him, her face fixed in a stony mask.

'OK, I'm sorry,' he mumbled, knowing that was exactly what Jenny was waiting for.

'You sound it,' she retorted briskly, picking up his coat from the chair and shaking the snow from it.

'I am. I may have a terrible reputation, and no doubt you would agree with it, but I happen to like animals— especially cats,' he added. 'God knows, on the family farm we're practically overrun by them,' he explained hurriedly, the conviction in his voice making her believe him.

She looked at him and was surprised by the tender expression on his usually ruthless face.

'You never struck me as a country boy,' she mocked, viewing him with curiosity at this revelation.

Thaddeus shrugged and looked strangely uncomfortable for a moment. 'I like to keep my private life private,' he said briskly.

'It's a pity you don't have the same respect for others,' she snapped back.

She watched him, hoping for a reaction, as he rubbed his hands together, trying to warm them, but he ignored the gibe as his eyes darted round the room.

'Where's the cat gone?' he asked, the tone of his voice betraying his concern. 'I am sorry about that,' he began again, his chiselled features softening in the warm, flickering glow of the fire.

'It's OK,' she said dismissively. 'It's not my cat anyway.' She shrugged as she took his coat in the hall to hang up. He followed her, and leant against the doorjamb, his figure still as daunting despite the casual stance.

'Not your cat?' he echoed in disbelief, acknowledging that she had goaded an apology from him for all his other behaviour.

'No, not my cat. Theo's a stray. Sometimes he appears when I come home, and stops for a couple of days, sometimes he doesn't. It's an ideal relationship—no commitment,' she added thoughtfully, unaware of the bitterness that had crept into her voice.

Thaddeus smiled slowly, his voice teasing as he drawled, 'That's how you like your relationships, Jennifer, is it? Not that I mean that as a criticism—on the contrary, I wish there were more women like you. Free, independent, not always demanding commitment.'

Jenny tried to ignore the effect he had on her whenever he said her name. She kept her inner turmoil well hidden, and her lips parted in a soft smile as she replied, 'That's a pretty cynical view, isn't it?' looking at him with cold distaste.

'Experience, that's all. I've never met a woman yet who doesn't want a band of gold. Despite all their protestations that it's just for laughs, sooner or later they start making demands,' he said with a tone of disgust.

'Well, rest assured, Mr Clarke, I'll be making no such demands on you,' she retorted briskly, annoyed by his arrogance—and yet his honesty surprised her. She

couldn't help but recall his dubious reputation. He had
fooled more than one female into believing he was ready
for marriage.

'I don't recall making you any such offer,' he bit back
through clenched teeth, his jaw tightening in disapproval. Jenny coloured slightly and turned away, but he
continued to goad her.

'You are capable of passion, I know,' he observed,
'but I can't be bothered chipping away at all that ice.
I'd love to meet the man responsible for your empty life,'
he continued as he watched her hanging up his coat.

Jenny spun round, her cheeks flushed with anger, and
met his mocking grin with a defiant tilt of her head.

'Thank you for your observations, but it's not something I want to discuss.' The edge in her voice was
brusque and firm. It told him quite clearly that it was
none of his business.

Thaddeus was unperturbed; his eyebrows rose mockingly but he remained silent and went back to the fire.
Jenny was grateful that he didn't question her further.
She wondered what he made of her statement about relationships. It was partly true—Jenny would have loved
to have relationships without commitment, to be as free
and easy as many of the girls she worked with—but she
couldn't. She had her own standards and she was going
to keep them, despite the pressures of her peers.

She returned to the lounge and felt a stab of anger
when she was met with the sight of Thaddeus. He was
a well-built man, lean yet muscular, and the revelation
that he had been brought up on a farm was confirmed
by his sturdy frame. There was something rugged about
him, despite the veneer of city life. He was sitting on

her most comfortable chair, pulling off his boots in a manner that suggested he was staying.

'What do you think you're doing?' she spat through gritted teeth. This was her domain, her home, and she resented his intrusion.

His head shot up and he pushed the swath of dark hair back from his face. His eyes glinted with amusement and he gave her a wicked smile. 'I should have thought it obvious,' he taunted. 'I'm taking my boots off,' he informed her, tossing them to one side and beginning to peel off his damp socks.

'You're not stopping here,' Jenny said as the realisation of the situation began to dawn.

He sighed wearily as he massaged his feet, trying to stir back some warmth into them. 'Well, I'm open to suggestions, but I've walked at least four miles to get here and there's nowhere else to stay,' he told her crisply. His deep blue eyes challenged her, and Jenny gave a tut of defeat. It was true, she was forced to admit—he would have to stay.

'I wouldn't throw a dog out on a night like this,' she agreed grudgingly as she picked up his boots and placed them on the hearth. Her cottage was far too small for untidiness, and suddenly it felt very cramped indeed.

'Thanks—from you I'll take that as a compliment. At least I rate higher than a dog,' he drawled, unperturbed by her caustic comment,.

'Only just, Mr Clarke. Only just,' she corrected with a smile as she went to fetch him a towel. There was a degree of smugness in her voice. She finally felt she had the upper hand. He watched her go and she could feel the weight of his eyes on her back; beads of perspiration immediately broke out and ran down her smooth skin.

Immediately her illusion of being in control evaporated. Jenny swallowed nervously as she drew a towel from the chest. She wasn't quite sure she wanted him here. He might be aware of her feelings towards him, and as yet she wasn't prepared to admit them even to herself. She wasn't prepared to get involved with a man who so blatantly acknowledged that he prized his freedom.

She strolled back into the cosy room and passed him a towel without comment. He took it with a grateful nod and began drying his mop of dark hair. Jenny went into the kitchen to prepare more vegetables—she had to feed him as well, she grumbled to herself as she peeled the potatoes.

'Can I help?' His warm velvet voice seemed to caress her, and she turned, unaware of the ready smile on her lips. He looked different here, less daunting, his size overwhelmed the tiny cottage, yet he seemed perfectly at peace here. The usual aggression and quick, fiery temper she knew suddenly seemed at odds with this man.

He cocked his head to one side, a boyish grin emphasising his dimples. He was wearing a checked shirt that was open at the collar to reveal a few tell-tale dark hairs. His jeans were so old that they had moulded themselves around his taut body, drawing attention to the sheer masculinity of the man.

'Well, do you want help?' he asked as Jenny remained silent, lost in her own thoughts. She quickly lowered her head and looked at his naked feet.

'You'd better not come in here. These tiles are lethal on bare skin,' she explained, then, seeing the look of disappointment on his face, she added quickly, 'You could set the table; it's the one in the corner,' and she nodded in the general direction.

'Thanks—it's like being at home. It was always my task to set the table,' he told her.

'Home?' Jenny echoed as she continued to prepare supper, shouting instructions out to Thaddeus about where everything was kept.

'Yes, on the farm; being the youngest, I rarely helped out with the animals. I stayed with my mother mostly,' he said, a dreamy, almost far-away wish in his voice.

'So you're the baby of the family.' She laughed; it was hard to imagine a man the size of Thaddeus as the smallest.

'That's right, and it was great. I was totally spoilt, not only by my two older brothers but by my sisters too,' he said as he looked at the array of books on Jenny's shelf.

'I read murder mysteries as well,' he acknowledged, pulling a book from the shelf and flicking through the pages. 'I can never solve them, can you?' he asked.

'No, never, but that's all part of the fun. Have you read the latest Detective Pagent story?' she asked eagerly, poking her head around the kitchen door. She was surprised that they shared the same taste in reading.

'Yes,' he nodded back with zeal. 'That double twist at the end really fooled me.' He pushed his damp hair from his face so that he could see her clearly.

'I couldn't sleep for a week after reading that. It was terrifying, and far too realistic,' she admitted, returning to the boiling vegetables.

'Shall I put on some music?' he called once he had finished looking over her book collection, but he didn't wait for a reply. He selected a popular piece of classical music and settled in the chair by the fire to listen to it.

It was some time later before Jenny finished cooking. She put the plates on the table then turned to see why he had not joined her. He lay slumped in the chair. Theo's forgiving nature had made him settle comfortably on Thaddeus's lap and they were both sound asleep. The flickering lights from the flames cast a warm glow on his features, softening them, and his sooty lashes curled gently up from his high cheeks.

He groaned softly and shifted in his chair. He was too big for it really; it was sheer exhaustion that had enabled him to sleep. Jenny jumped as he moved and suddenly realised that she could so easily have been caught staring at him. She shook his shoulder roughly and snapped sharply in an attempt to conceal her soft nature. He jumped, immediately alert, his eyes wide and as blue as the sky.

'What is it?' he demanded, confused for a moment, and his eyes darted quickly around as he assessed where he was. He sank back down with a sigh.

'Dinner,' barked Jenny, seating herself at the table. It was too small for two and it gave an intimacy to their meal that she didn't like. It made her feel self-conscious as he sat down opposite her with an ease that unnerved her still further.

Thaddeus refilled her wine glass and Jenny nodded her thanks as she ladled the hot stew on to his plate. He ate in silence and Jenny was secretly pleased. The lack of conversation was not due to embarrassment but to his preoccupation with the food. He ate every morsel with obvious pleasure. It was a simple meal: a selection of vegetables, fresh dinner rolls and a beef stew. Jenny ate little, toying with the fluffy herb dumplings and pushing her vegetables about her plate. She caught

Thaddeus's eyes watching her but was unable to read the expression on his face as she concentrated on her plate.

'That was delicious,' he said, finally pushing his plate away. He put his knife and fork down, his plate completely empty. 'Real home cooking—I miss that.'

'Hunger is a sweet sauce,' she reminded him, not wanting him to see she was pleased by his flattery. He raised his dark-winged brows and shook his head.

'Are you always so touchy when complimented?' He laughed. His features were gentle and playful and Jenny stiffened as she tried to remain aloof from him. She frowned and snapped back nastily,

'You forget I've seen you in action. Flattery may get you what you want of most women, but not me.' Her voice was antagonistic and her expression equally hostile.

He studied her carefully for a few moments, taking the full impact of her flashing eyes as she waited for battle to commence. Instead his grin widened still further, revealing his perfect white teeth. He leant over the table, the only barrier between them, and took her hand.

'Jennifer,' he almost whispered, the silky pronunciation of her name sending a shiver of delight through her body. She struggled to remain immune to his seductive charm. 'You know me so well that I see little reason for pretence,' he said, wrapping his hand over hers, tracing her throbbing wrist pulses with his thumb. The cool stroke was sending a riot of feelings through Jenny, feelings that had been dormant for so long that it hurt to suddenly be aware of them again. She drew her hand back as if she had been scorched, her body tense with anger at her own weakness.

'What do you want?' she demanded, not wanting him to toy with her emotions. She tried to control the treacherous betrayal of her body, yet her heart still beat furiously at the memory of his scorching touch. He shrugged lazily, but the strength of the man was still apparent in every gesture.

'I want you to come to Tunisia,' he stated bluntly. Jenny was on her feet in seconds, her face set grimly.

'I could have saved you the trouble of coming here...' she began, her voice remarkably calm considering how she felt. He, too, was on his feet with an animal agility that excited and frightened her at the same time. She stepped back, putting a greater distance between them, but she instinctively knew it was not far enough.

'Saved me the trouble?' he yelled scornfully, viewing her with angry disdain. 'You have been nothing but trouble. Had you had the decency to answer my call I shouldn't have had to waste my time journeying up to this hell-hole,' he bellowed; his features were suddenly sharp again and distorted with anger. A pulse throbbed with a steady rhythm in his temple and Jenny's eyes were drawn to it.

She watched it with grim fascination before retorting angrily, 'This hell-hole, as you call it, happens to be my home, and as you have now been given the answer you came for I suggest you leave.' She stormed towards the door, determined to have him out, but he pulled her back roughly and pushed her down into a chair. She tried to get up, but his eyes froze her to the spot. They were burning with an icy flame that cut into her soul, trapping her in their drowning depths.

'I haven't driven and walked all this way for a negative response and I've no intention of going anywhere till you agree to come to Tunisia.' His voice was low and threatening and he stood, blocking her route of escape.

She had never seen him so angry; he raised his hand to rake it through his hair in frustration and Jenny's eyes were drawn to the movement as she sat transfixed. Her mind was racing with terrible thoughts: she was alone with a man who would stop at nothing to achieve his own ends. The cottage was isolated and they were cut off... the scenario was better suited to a horror movie, she thought, suddenly frantic.

'You haven't a choice; you know the situation at work. The management are insisting on cutbacks to stay in business. You come on this job or you're out,' he ground out, an edge of triumph in his voice.

Jenny struggled to remain calm. She couldn't afford to lose her job; she had to pay the mortgage on her cottage—she couldn't lose that. She looked at him with contempt apparent in every detail of her face. How she hated him, the power he had over her—yet she knew there was no alternative.

'I have to come, then,' she said quietly with resignation in her voice.

There was a sudden flash of emotion on his face that she couldn't quite discern. He mumbled a curse and turned his back, walking over to the window and drawing back the curtains to gaze out across the barren desolation.

'You make it sound like an ordeal. It doesn't have to be; it could be fun,' he said, turning to face her again. Jenny shrugged her shoulders, knowing full well that for her it would be a terrible ordeal. There seemed little point in discussing it further. Jenny knew she had no option and she couldn't blame Thaddeus entirely. Yet she still had an uneasy feeling about the whole thing, as if he was keeping something from her.

*   *   *

Three days later, at eight o'clock at night, Jenny and Thaddeus landed at Tunis-Carthage Airport. The black velvet sky was covered with a myriad sequin stars twinkling in the far distance.

They descended the aircraft steps and Jenny gave a gasp as the hot air hit her. The heat was rising from the ground and the air was hot and unbearably stifling. Jenny was grateful that they were through Passport Control in minutes.

It was a large modern airport and the place was teeming with people. The moment Jenny and Thaddeus were spotted as potential customers, a stream of youths followed them, all eager to carry their luggage or to get them a taxi. The air was heavy with the sweet, over-powering smell of jasmine as the youths thrust small nosegays at Jenny, begging her to buy one. Thaddeus wasted no time—pushing everyone aside, he quickly ordered a taxi to take them to their hotel.

The drive to the hotel took only a short time, but the experience was unforgettable to Jenny. She gazed out of the window, watching the passing scenes with cries of delight. The street cafés were alive with people—mostly men, she noted. Then she remembered it was a Muslim country; women would hardly be likely to be out at night.

They were booked into a luxury hotel on the Avenue Habib Bourguiba. It was an immensely long street stretching from the port on Lake Tunis to the Place de l'Indépendance. Jenny was glad to be out of the taxi and inside the hotel, where the air-conditioning cooled the air.

'Take a shower and then we shall have dinner,' Thaddeus said, tossing her room-key towards her. Jenny caught it deftly and smiled, feeling more that she was

on holiday than working. Yet she was determined to keep
this on a purely professional level. Thaddeus had been
polite throughout the journey, but the intimacy and
friendship that had nearly developed at the cottage now
seemed like a dream, and Jenny wondered if she had
imagined it all.

She opened her bedroom door and switched on the
light. It was a lovely room. A huge bed dominated it,
already folded back, and the crisp, pure white cotton
sheets seemed to be calling her travel-weary body to rest.
But Jenny dismissed the idea; she was not on holiday,
she reminded herself, and it was obvious she and
Thaddeus had a great deal of work ahead of them.

She took a quick shower, allowing the clean force of
the water to awaken her tired limbs. Then she flung open
her suitcase and pulled a simple cotton dress from it.
She had had the dress for years; it was pale blue, very
plain, with an embroidered lace trim for the collar. She
slipped into it and frowned. She had not worn it since
her last holiday, but it had always fitted her! She went
over to the mirror and stared in disbelief. The dress
looked so different. It had always fallen over her loosely,
a typical sundress and ideal for hot climates. Not now;
it seemed to hug her body with an alarming snugness.
The embroidered collar traced around her breasts,
drawing attention to them. The fall of the dress was different, too—instead of the loose sack it had been, it emphasised her slim waist and made her hips look well
rounded and firm.

Jenny tried to swallow the rising bile at the back of
her throat as she saw her own reflection. She had the
figure of a woman, and a nervous rush of perspiration
broke out on her back. She suddenly felt very self-

conscious, and would have changed immediately had there not been a sharp rap on the door.

'Ready?' called Thaddeus in a voice that warned her he was in no mood to wait.

'Coming,' she answered, snatching up a shawl and throwing it around herself to disguise her dress.

The restaurant in the hotel served predominantly French food and Thaddeus viewed the menu like a connoisseur, enjoying the array of dishes. Jenny wasn't sure what to do; she certainly felt hungry, but she had obviously gained weight.

'Are you wearing anything under that shawl?' asked Thaddeus, laughing as she coloured. 'You might as well wear a tent. You're not going native on me, are you?' he laughed, again good-humouredly. 'We've only just arrived.'

Jenny bristled with annoyance and flung the shawl back from her shoulders with a gesture of impatience. 'Of course not,' she snapped angrily. 'It's just that I seem to have gained weight and——' She stopped as Thaddeus interrupted.

'In all the right places,' he murmured hoarsely, his eyes travelling over her with a slowness that alarmed her. His eyes seemed to burn a trail across her body, and Jenny felt a rush of colour to her face. 'You look wonderful,' he said smokily, smiling at her.

Jenny flushed again and lowered her head, embarrassed by his blatant appraisal. He leaned over the table, taking her chin with his fingers and forcing her to meet his penetrating gaze.

'What's the matter?' he asked, sensing something was wrong. She tried to move her head to turn away but he would not allow her to. 'I meant it as a compliment,' he reassured her, and Jenny's eyes flicked to his, searching for sincerity and startled when she found it.

'You don't think I look fat?' she questioned him quietly, looking around to ensure no one was listening. His face broke into a wide smile, and his shoulders shook as he tried to suppress his laughter.

'You're not fat, you're shapely,' he insisted, catching her hand in a gesture of friendship. He could contain his laughter no longer and he erupted noisily. 'You eat like a sparrow; how could you possibly be fat?' he spluttered.

Jenny was forced to join in his laughter as the truth of his words sank deep into her mind. She had been aware of a change herself, but to have it confirmed by someone was so very reassuring. It was like being reborn, and her heart soared to dizzy heights as she realised she wasn't in the least bit overweight—or underweight. Jenny looked at the menu with renewed interest. Her days of self-denial were over, and she was going to enjoy life.

Thaddeus sat quietly as Jenny made her order. She ignored the waiter's suggestion of a salad, and instead ordered the selection of vegetables. Thaddeus smiled, a little bemused by her behaviour, and he watched her closely as she ate with obvious enjoyment.

'I presume you have reached your target weight after dieting and this is your reward,' he mentioned casually, unprepared for her reaction. Jenny froze, her eyes suddenly wide and her face a myriad emotions—anger, sorrow, disgust. Thaddeus stared in disbelief as her cutlery dropped from her hands and she rushed out of the restaurant.

Jenny didn't know where to run—she just knew she had to put as much distance as she could between her and Thaddeus Clarke. He had been right, of course; that was what hurt. She was rewarding herself, and she hated that. She hated the fact that she still used food as some sort of bargaining coin. She resented even more the fact that she wanted to be acceptable to Thaddeus. He had approved of her, and that had made her feel good about herself. Jenny shuddered. She had taken that route before, seeing herself only as a reflection through a man's eyes.

She fled from the hotel, her mind in a turmoil as she tried to rationalise her fears. The temperature had fallen and she gave a shiver as the cool wind whipped against her body. It was dark outside, but a path in the garden was quite well lit and she hurried down it. She wanted to hide, deep down and far away where no one could find her.

She sat on a bench at the far end of the garden. The night air was heavy with the strong scent of jasmine and the crickets sang in ever-increasing chorus in the dark undergrowth. Jenny rubbed her bare arms with her hands—in her haste to leave she had forgotten her shawl. She felt such a fool, and what on earth would Thaddeus make of her behaviour? She knew she had over-reacted, yet every moment seemed intensified in Thaddeus's company.

'I think you owe me an explanation.' A cool voice shattered the silence. Thaddeus dropped her shawl around her shivering shoulders in a disdainful gesture.

Jenny jumped; she had been so absorbed in her own thoughts that she had not heard him approach. He seemed to have suddenly materialised as if created out of her own thoughts. She said nothing, but kept her eyes lowered, staring at the red dust at her feet, fascinated by the intricate dance of a pair of ants.

'I'm waiting.' His voice was sharp. The well-hidden edge of anger still managed to cut through the still night air.

Jenny flicked her eyes upwards, without raising her head, and caught a quick look at him. He seemed to have grown at least an inch. He towered above her, his face set with determination and his eyes blazing. He sank his hands deep into his jacket, and the sudden movement made Jenny flinch. He sat beside her. He seemed troubled, but his face remained as harsh as ever. His jaw clenched as he snapped at her in a low voice, 'What did you do that for?' his eyes flaring with unspent passion.

Jenny shook her head, unable to confront the wrath on his face, too bewildered to answer him.

'What's going on, Jennifer?' he demanded, sitting beside her, his body inflexible and unmoving. Jenny knew there was little chance of escaping his questioning. His attitude was resolute, and he was far too astute to allow her any falsehoods.

'It's private, personal. It has nothing to do with you,' she mumbled, disliking his proximity as it only increased her sense of vulnerability. She could sense the unleashed anger in the stiff line of his body and the steady throbbing of the temple in his head.

'It damn well is. Imagine what people thought when you fled the room, a look of fear and panic on your face,' he cut in. 'Then I had to pretend it was all perfectly normal while they laughed at me at best, or looked at me as if I were the devil incarnate!' he finished stonily.

Jenny allowed herself a grin in the darkness of the garden. She would have liked to see that, she admitted silently to herself; but her moment of pleasure was short-lived as Thaddeus grabbed her hard by the shoulders and twisted her round to face him.

She stared open-mouthed at the dark fury on his face, the storm that was building with a cold ruthlessness in his eyes. She tried to pull away but his grip merely tightened till she could feel his fingers sinking into her soft skin. She gave a cry, but it was quickly stifled by the warning look on his face.

'Let go,' Jenny pleaded desperately, but he shook his head slowly and she knew she was defeated.

'I want to know what's going on. You're so tense, your appetite is pathetic and the moment you're complimented on your figure you order food as if it's going out of fashion. Then no sooner does your order arrive than you run away like a scalded cat. I just don't understand—what is it with you?'

She knew he already had suspicions. He was quicker than most—far more perceptive, just as Margaret had been—not that she'd thanked her for it. Jenny sighed, suddenly feeling very weary.

'I was anorexic,' she confessed, her words hanging in the air like a fly trapped in honey. She saw him stiffen, felt him draw back, but dared not look at his face—his disgust would be too much to bear.

The silence between them was like an impenetrable wall till he broke down all her fears and anxieties with the words, 'Can I help?'

Jenny's head shot up; she couldn't believe what she had just heard, and felt sure he had misheard her.

'I said I was anorexic,' she said again clearly, her voice gaining strength as she realised maybe he had understood.

'I heard you the first time,' he replied, a smile playing on his lips. 'But you're not any more, are you?' he said confidently. His face was lit by the shadowy light from the hotel; his eyes, though serious, were gentle, and there was an understanding in them that she had not expected to see.

'No, I'm not any more, not really. I don't avoid food or try to make myself sick.' She paused, wondering whether she was disgusting him, but his expression was bland; only his eyes held a flicker of interest. 'I still don't eat enough but my appetite is improving all the time and it's nearly normal now. I admit to being anorexic so that I never forget I nearly died.'

She heard his sudden intake of breath and wondered if she had said too much, but he remained quiet, waiting for her to continue her story. 'I was pulled back from the brink, but I never thanked the person responsible— at the time I thought she was wrong and I was right,' Jenny admitted with sorrow.

'Why, Jenny? There always is a reason. What was yours?' he asked quietly, and Jenny sank her head into her hands and began to sob. No one but her sister had ever shown any real concern about her illness, and she could never tell her sister the root cause. It would have been too painful for both of them.

Thaddeus wrapped his arm around her shoulders and drew her towards his chest. She fell against it, enjoying the strong, steady beat of his heart as it thudded through her ears. She stayed there, crying away all the pain and hurt she had been through, and he said nothing, just rocked her and smoothed her thick mantle of hair from her face as it stuck there with her hot, salty tears.

'We'd best go inside,' he whispered. 'I'll come to your room and you can tell me all about it.'

Jenny rose to her feet in a dream-like state and leant heavily on Thaddeus as he escorted her back into the hotel. He placed her gently on her bed, which sank considerably as he sat down beside her.

'I want the full story,' he said, his dark eyes fixing on her. She was no longer going to be allowed to hide behind her veil of tears; he wanted to know. Jenny swallowed hard and hoped she could tell him without revealing too much. She looked up and faced him, suddenly no longer afraid.

CHAPTER FIVE

JENNY faltered for a moment. She wasn't sure where to begin. It all seemed so long ago now, as if it had all happened to someone else. She knew Thaddeus was waiting, trying to keep a close rein on his formidable temper. She caught the look of growing impatience in his eyes, the throbbing nerve at his temple as he drew his hair back from his face.

'Come on, Jenny,' he said quietly. 'I want to know.'

Jenny couldn't help but wonder why he was interested—unless it was something to do with the job. She felt tired now, too tired to talk; her emotions had all been spent—but Thaddeus was waiting and she knew there was no chance of sleep till she told him. He sat beside her, tapping his feet in a gesture of impatience, and Jenny swallowed, still unsure of his reaction.

'My father remarried when I was twelve. My only sister's career began to take off at the same time and I felt very unloved and unwanted,' she began, her voice trembling with emotion. 'My sister tried to help as much as she could, but she was so beautiful that I always felt ugly. I ate for comfort. I ate and ate and ate and by the time I was sixteen I was huge—four stones overweight.' Her shoulders sank wearily with the weight of the memory. Thaddeus sat silently beside her, stroking his long fingers on the strong length of his leg as he listened attentively.

'Did no one try to help?' he asked, quietly annoyed, a mental image of how unhappy she must have been flashing through his mind.

'Yes,' mumbled Jenny, barely audible, 'but I enjoyed food and I gave the impression that I was happy with my weight,' she confessed, hating herself for having been so foolish and joining in the laughter when she was the butt of people's jokes. The memories were still as bitter even now.

'So how did you change from being overweight to becoming anorexic?' he demanded tightly, his voice low and grim, his lids lowered to hide his emotion.

'I fell in love,' she stated simply, unaware of the flash of light in Thaddeus's eyes and the slight stiffening of his body. 'I fell hopelessly head over heels and he loved me—or at least...' She paused as the pain ripped through her chest, making it impossible for her to continue. Thaddeus threw a protective arm around her instantly, holding her close, trying to absorb her pain.

Jenny drew strength from him and she suffocated her tears in order to continue. 'I was very young, very foolish. I was flattered by his attention and so very scared of losing him. I would have done anything for him. He said he didn't care about my size. It was more of me to love, he said, and I believed him.' She shook her head dismally, as if the very idea was stupid.

'But he dumped you,' interjected Thaddeus as he began to understand the pathetic story. His voice was serious and matched his expression perfectly. Jenny nodded dumbly as hot pins of pain stabbed the back of her eyes, willing herself not to cry. She swallowed nervously.

'Yes—yes, he did. I guess at the time it was all just too much. I was seeing less and less of my sister because she had work commitments. My father was so besotted with his young wife that he never even considered me, and my exams were on the horizon. It just all got too much for me,' she confessed slowly.

'That's a hell of a lot of pressure for one kid,' he said softly.

'I began to diet, to try and win him back, to get my father's attention, to look like my sister. There were so many reasons, and all of them seem pretty silly now. My sister told me not to, that I was being too drastic, but I no longer saw myself as others did. I stopped eating, fasted for days, but it made no difference. He no longer wanted me, I'd lost him—and she was partly to blame,' Jenny added with a stab of bitterness.

'Who was to blame?' asked Thaddeus, catching her tone and realising there was something more.

'My sister,' she spat. 'She's ten years older than me and I worshipped her—everyone does. She couldn't understand what it was like to be fat and ugly,' she sobbed again, falling against his hard chest till the shirt he was wearing clung to his body, revealing the dark whorls of rugged hair that matted his chest. 'She told me I was foolish, but she didn't have to live in my shadow as I always lived in hers. We had a huge row. Looking back, I can see it wasn't her fault, but I blamed her, blamed her for everything. I think Paul just used me as a stepping-stone to her, but I blamed her. I'm so sorry now,' she sobbed again, and Thaddeus wiped the tears from her eyes with his white silk handkerchief. He couldn't quite understand what had brought on this torrent of emotion.

Jenny sat on the bed, numb. It seemed so strange talking about herself like that; she had never confided in anyone before, and the relief was immense. She was glad, though, that she would be back in England once the filming began. She knew now she could not bear to see Pablo.

Thaddeus ran her a scented bath, showing her a tenderness that she did not expect. She would have objected, but the steely look in his eyes silenced her. He allowed her to soak gently till the pain and anger had all but dissolved away.

'Come on, let's have you out of there,' he called firmly at last as he waited by the door. Jenny obeyed immediately. She didn't know how he had taken her revelation. He had remained completely silent throughout her confession, his expression unreadable. She wrapped herself up in the thick warm towel and came back into the bedroom.

Thaddeus was sitting by the window, gazing out on the twinkling lights of Tunis. He was deep in thought and a frown of concentration furrowed his brow. Jenny pulled the towel even tighter around her as he turned and saw her. She was suddenly aware of her state of undress and his gaze seemed to pass over her with a depth of vision that worried her. A pot of strong sweet coffee and an array of sandwiches was waiting for her, and Jenny smiled gratefully as she slipped on to the chair opposite him.

'You look better,' he commented approvingly as he watched her take up a sandwich. Jenny smiled. She certainly felt better—except for his proximity.

'Confession is good for the soul,' she admitted, suddenly feeling better, as if a huge burden had been lifted from her shoulders. Her face was filled with gratitude and her lips parted softly. 'Thank you,' she said quietly, gazing into Thaddeus's eyes. He looked at her and their eyes met. For a moment it was if time itself stood still. They were locked into immobility. Jenny recovered first, lowering her eyes and toying with her coffee-cup.

'We shall go sightseeing tomorrow to get a feel of the place. Track down government offices so we know where to apply for any official clearances,' Thaddeus said briskly, shattering the moment which they had shared but which neither of them understood.

'Well, I'd best get to bed—I'm exhausted. It must be all the travelling,' said Jenny, suddenly wanting him to go. She had been hurt by his businesslike tone and the fact that he had destroyed something very beautiful between them. He didn't argue, which increased her disappointment. Instead he rose with alarming speed, as if he longed to be out of her company.

'Goodnight, Jennifer,' he called as he left, and the door closed with a click.

Jenny felt more alone than she had ever done in her life. She stared at the door as a familiar wave of rejection came over her. She climbed into bed wearily, her mind in a turmoil but too tired to think.

Jenny tossed the crumpled linen sheet away from her body. It had entangled itself around her leg, making her feel so uncomfortable that she had awoken early.

She knew it was going to be hot today—very hot. Her soft skin was already tingling with the prickly sense of heat. The azure sky was completely cloudless and the sun was already high, though it was barely past six o'clock.

Jenny groaned as she pushed the sheets from her body. She had not slept well all night. Probably due to the heat, she told herself, but deep down inside she knew the real cause. It was the overwhelming sense of loneliness that had taken her over since Thaddeus had left.

She decided to have a cool shower to rid herself of the oppressive sleep that still clung to her. The sound of running water filled the luxurious bathroom and Jenny stepped under the pounding water with a squeal. The gushing water swept over her body, washing away the remnants of sleep, and she shampooed her hair with the ivy-scented body shampoo till her scalp tingled. The soft soapsuds cascaded over her firm breasts before falling on to her flat stomach.

Her hand moved across her body as if she were experiencing it for the first time. She gave a secret smile as she tossed her head back and allowed the water to fall with its full impact on her face. The torrent was hard and unrelenting, and she closed her eyes tightly against its onslaught. She felt as if she was being baptised, re-born a new person who was finally happy with the way she looked. She knew the past was behind her and looked forward to a brighter future.

She dressed with care, suddenly feeling good about herself. She longed for a new image to go with her new feeling of confidence. She promised herself a shopping trip for some new outfits as soon as possible.

As she descended the stairs of the hotel she suddenly remembered Thaddeus. How could she face him? she thought frantically. She had revealed more to him than to any other living soul and the implications of that frightened her.

It took considerable effort to present a relaxed façade as he approached her. He had obviously been waiting for her in the foyer, and he rose to greet her the moment he saw her.

Jenny paused momentarily and swallowed hard. He moved with such animal grace, despite his size. She was aware of the masculinity and the threat he posed to her equilibrium as he grew closer. She felt a flipping sensation in her stomach as he stopped in front of her. She felt quite intimidated by him, but she refused to let him see it: she spoke to him with amazing composure, although her insides were such a mass of nerves.

'Good morning. I hope you slept well,' she said, flicking her sheaf of wheat-coloured hair back from her face in an attempt to appear indifferent to him.

'As always, Jennifer—and you?' There was infinite mockery beneath his polite veneer, and Jenny could hear the laughter in his voice.

'Yes, thank you,' she retorted sharply. She had not wanted this; she had hoped for more. Instead it was obvious it was business as usual. 'I'm ready to start work as soon as you are,' she added firmly. She wanted to reinforce their business relationship immediately.

His eyebrows rose and the full impact of his blue eyes seared her soul.

'Breakfast first, don't you think?' The offer seemed sincere enough, but Jenny couldn't help but wonder if he was goading her. However, it didn't really matter, as breakfast was a simple affair and Jenny ate as much as Thaddeus.

'I've booked us on a tour this morning. I didn't think we would be up to anything too strenuous, and you'll be able to jot down anything you think suitable,' he informed her crisply as they left the dining-room. Jenny nodded and hurried upstairs to grab her notebook and pens. Her heart was racing and she leant against the door, breathless and agitated. What on earth had happened to her? She felt marvellous, totally alive. She rushed back down just as everyone was boarding the coach and slipped into the seat next to Thaddeus.

He turned and frowned. 'Go and sit over there on the other side, then we'll both see a different aspect,' he growled, then turned away abruptly and gazed out of his window.

Jenny flushed at his sharpness, but knew he was right. It was the only sensible thing to do. She sat at the window, reminding herself that she was at work, not on holiday, and that her relationship with Thaddeus was purely professional. Yet somehow she couldn't help but feel disappointed.

Finally, after an extensive tour around Tunis, the coach stopped. Everyone alighted and took separate paths to see the parts that interested them. The majority of them made their way to the Porte de France, the gateway to the Medina. This was the oldest part of town—a shoppers' paradise.

Jenny decided not to wait for Thaddeus; if she found anywhere suitable she could tell him later. She didn't want him to tell her what to do again. She began to walk slowly to the Medina. Several different little boys immediately hurried towards her. They held out nosegays and demanded and pleaded for her to have one. The sultry heavy perfume of jasmine hung in the air, and Jenny would have bought one, but she wanted to see the Medina first. As the oldest part of town it would probably be ideal for some shots.

However, the word 'no' and a shake of the head was not enough. They followed her relentlessly, heedless of her refusals. Jenny was becoming tired of their insistence, and when one of them finally thrust a nosegay in her face her patience broke.

'Go away!' she snapped, her vision impaired by the dark sunglasses she was wearing.

'I have no intention of going away,' a level voice informed her, and Jenny lowered her glasses to look at the familiar smiling face of Thaddeus. Her stomach flipped as she felt the warmth of his smile.

'I'm going to the Medina,' she said, amazed at the calmness of her voice. His proximity was driving her wild. It was hard to maintain complete composure under his steady gaze.

'Then I shall come with you,' he said, taking her arm in a firm grip that brooked no argument. Jenny soon fell into pace with him.

'Thank you for the flowers,' she said, toying with the delicate pink and white blooms secured together with a silk ribbon. She couldn't bear to look at him; she knew her feelings could no longer be hidden. She loved him, and she did not want him to know: his rejection would be more than she could bear.

'Do you like the scent of jasmine? It was bought by way of an apology,' he explained, his deep voice sending a thrill of excitement through her body. 'I was a little sharp before,' he added by way of explanation, but he said no more, just smiled, the same earth-shattering smile that made Jenny feel weak at the knees. It must be the heat, she mused to herself, or the intoxicating aroma of the jasmine—but both explanations seemed a little lame.

'You think the Medina will have some interesting shots?' he asked as their pace increased.

'Yes, I do, but there are several other places. The embassy, for one, looks as if it's straight from the *Arabian Nights*,' she said, nodding in the direction of an elaborately decorated building.

Thaddeus stopped dead in his tracks, his intelligent blue eyes making a swift and complete inventory of the building. 'Camera,' he barked out, stretching his arm, and Jenny obeyed immediately. He took several shots from various angles, though they both knew permission would still have to be granted if they wanted to use even the façade for shots. They continued making their way to the Medina, both of them taking in every nook and cranny, trying to picture it in a scene.

The main street of the Medina was called Rue Djama ez Zitouna, and the moment they walked down it the impact was immediate. It was like stepping back in time. They were surrounded by a whole host of different things, each one assailing their senses, demanding attention—the vivid colours, brilliant copper, rusty iron, blazing brass, shining jewellery. A kaleidoscope of metal colours all mingling with the musical sound of the craftsmen's incessant hammering.

'This is great!' marvelled Thaddeus, his eyes quickly scanning the scene and mentally adding his own characters. The rich smell of roasting lamb enticed them further in and the air seemed to be filled with a mixture of aromas, of roasting coffee-beans as well as spices and herbs and heavy scented oils. For a few moments they walked round together, commenting periodically on the fascinating scenes.

Jenny never stopped taking photographs, and she drew attention to herself by her actions. A young Arab man from a perfume counter called her over and she smiled as he offered to make her a perfume to entice her husband. She blushed then, and tried to move away, but the young man was insistent. Thaddeus drew up at the side of her, his body stiff and aggressive.

'What's he saying?' he demanded, noting Jenny's flushed face. She shook her head, too embarrassed to tell him. Thaddeus grabbed her roughly by the arm and drew her away. 'What did he want?' he growled, the grip on her arm so tight that she flinched, but he made no attempt to release her.

'He wanted to make me a perfume, to *entice my husband*,' she snapped, outraged by his strange behaviour. She was no longer embarrassed, just angry.

'What made him think we were married?'

'Because we are together, unchaperoned, and this is a Muslim country.'

The look of relief on Thaddeus's face annoyed Jenny, and she pulled away from him, rubbing her arm with deliberation. He remained silent and she stole a glance at him. He seemed deep in thought, far away, and they left the Medina in silence.

'Let's go and have a drink,' he suggested. A smile broke out on Jenny's face until he added, 'We have a lot to discuss.'

She nodded understandingly as the hot pinheads pricked the back of her eyes. She hated herself for her own self-delusion. She had seen it so often: working long, unsociable hours for any length of time tended to throw people together. It was so much easier to imagine yourself in love.

Jenny sighed and wished she had heeded her own advice. She couldn't work Thaddeus out. He changed so quickly from being her best friend to the director, in less than a blink of an eye.

'I've brought you a lemonade,' he said as he placed the tall glass down on the table and moved his chair under the umbrella, out of the sun's bright rays.

'We shall have to do very early morning shots; this heat will be unbearable by eleven,' Jenny offered as she sipped her drink, aware that eyes were on her.

'Mmm,' he said, obviously uninterested, and Jenny's eyes flashed to his. Again there it was, a magical moment for her when time seemed suspended. She knew she was blushing and her heart-rate had increased. She wished he wouldn't look at her like that. There was something in his eyes, a hunger that pleased and frightened her at the same time.

'Let's go back to the hotel. I've a few calls to make and we can meet up later,' he said sharply, his voice guarded and his gaze suddenly troubled. Jenny nodded and gave a sigh. She suddenly felt very tired, and the thought of resting while he made some calls was instantly appealing.

The heat of the day was increasing as they made their way back to the hotel. The cool air-conditioning that greeted them was most welcome.

'Let's meet in about an hour,' Thaddeus suggested crisply as he passed her her door-key.

'Fine.' Jenny nodded back. 'Have you any plans?' she asked, curious to know what he had in mind. His face lit with a brilliant smile, dazzling her till she felt her pulse race.

'You arrange car hire and I'll take you somewhere very special,' he said with a wicked grin. 'And bring some beachwear,' he added with a wink.

Jenny took the stairs two at a time. The tiredness had left her and she was looking forward to the opportunity of a little sunbathing. She grabbed her swimsuit from the wardrobe and snatched up a towel, flinging them carelessly into her beach-bag along with a bottle of sun-oil. Though she didn't burn easily, it had been a long time since she had been in the sun. She tried hard not to get too excited; she had to remain conscious of the fact that she was still here to work.

Hiring a car was surprisingly easy and Jenny was pleased that she managed to slip into speaking French with such ease. She lay on her bed, listening to the noise of the busy street below, waiting impatiently for the hour to pass so she could be away. She was really looking forward to this afternoon. At last the time arrived and she hurried downstairs. Thaddeus greeted her with a smile.

'I see you've managed to arrange transport,' he said, the approval in his voice making her heart leap, though Jenny tried to not be affected by his high opinion of her. They drove along the open coast roads, miles upon miles of almost derelict land. Occasionally incongruous modern buildings suddenly marred the desolation.

'Where are we going?' Jenny asked as she stared out of the window, enjoying the stark landscape.

Thaddeus smiled.

'Surely you've seen the posters?' he asked teasingly, enjoying the pensive frown that furrowed Jenny's face as she thought hard. She shook her head.

NO COST! NO OBLIGATION TO BUY!
NO PURCHASE NECESSARY!

PLAY "LUCKY 7"
AND GET AS MANY AS SIX FREE GIFTS...

HOW TO PLAY:

1 With a coin, carefully scratch off the silver box opposite. You will now be eligible to receive two or more FREE books, and possibly other gifts, depending on what is revealed beneath the scratch off area.

2 When you return this card, you'll receive specially selected Mills & Boon Romances. We'll send you the books and gifts you qualify for absolutely FREE, and at the same time we'll reserve you a subscription to our Reader Service.

3 If we don't hear from you within 10 days, we'll then send you four brand new Romances to read and enjoy every month for just £1.80 each, the same price as the books in the shops. There is no extra charge for postage and handling. There are no hidden extras.

4 When you join the Mills & Boon Reader Service, you'll also get our free monthly Newsletter, featuring author news, horoscopes, penfriends and competitions.

5 You are under no obligation, and may cancel or suspend your subscription at any time simply by writing to us.

You'll love your cuddly teddy. His brown eyes and cute face are sure to make you smile.

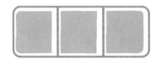

Play "Lucky 7"

Just scratch off the silver box with a coin.
Then check below to see which gifts you get.

YES! I have scratched off the silver box. Please send me all the gifts for which I qualify. I understand that I am under no obligation to purchase any books, as explained on the opposite page. I am over 18 years of age.

6A3R

MS/MRS/MISS/MR _____

ADDRESS _____

_____

POSTCODE _____ SIGNATURE _____

7 7 7	**WORTH FOUR FREE BOOKS** **FREE TEDDY BEAR AND MYSTERY GIFT**
🔔 🔔 🔔	**WORTH FOUR FREE BOOKS** **AND MYSTERY GIFT**
🍒 🍒 🍒	**WORTH FOUR FREE BOOKS**
🍒 🔔 BAR	**WORTH TWO FREE BOOKS**

MILLS & BOON "NO RISK" GUARANTEE

* You're not required to buy a single book!

* You must be completely satisfied or you may cancel at any time simply by writing to us. You will receive no more books; you'll have no further obligation.

* The free books and gifts you receive from this offer remain yours to keep no matter what you decide.

If offer details are missing, write to:
Mills & Boon Reader Service, P.O. Box 236, Croydon, Surrey CR9 9EL

Mills & Boon Reader Service
FREEPOST
P.O. Box 236
Croydon
Surrey
CR9 9EL

NO
STAMP
NEEDED

'No, I can't say I have,' she retorted briskly, curiosity eating away at her.

'We are going to Sidi Bou Said,' he informed her, pleased by the instant recognition that flashed through her eyes. Jenny gave a gasp of pleasure.

'Of course I've seen the posters—it looks marvellous,' she agreed enthusiastically.

Sidi Bou Said was a tiny village situated high up on a hill. Thaddeus parked the car on the roadside with care and placed a sun-shield up against the windscreen.

'It will be stiflingly hot,' he explained to Jenny, and she nodded in agreement—the sun *was* extremely hot.

They began to walk through the tiny picturesque village. The houses were like a million sugar cubes stacked neatly on top of one another. The wood-workers' art was clear to see, the intricate minarets and tiny castle-like designs. Jenny photographed the blue-doored white houses with delight; the delicate fretwork windows were an ideal method of air-conditioning in the tiny houses.

'Do you want a drink?' Thaddeus offered, his voice sounding weary, and Jenny flashed him a look.

'The weather too hot for you?' she asked, noticing the heated look on his face and the damp beads of perspiration on his forehead. He frowned as if angered that she should see a weakness in him.

'Yes,' he snapped irritably, crossing the road to a small bar, not even waiting for her. Jenny followed—she too was hot, and the thought of a cold drink was welcoming.

'What's this?' asked Jenny warily as she watched a wizened old man ramming vast quantities of green leaves and sugar into a squat curvy pewter pot. She could hear the water boiling inside and frowned. 'I really wanted a cool drink,' she said to Thaddeus, ignoring the look of contempt on his face.

'This will be more refreshing, I assure you,' he informed her crisply as she slid into the stool beside him.

'I'm quite capable of choosing what I want to drink,' she retorted quickly, annoyed by his high-handed attitude.

'No doubt you are, but on this occasion you have not been given a choice.' The grim finality in his voice told Jenny that the conversation was at an end, and she forced a smile as a glass of the hot brown liquid was passed to her. She viewed it askance for a moment but, catching the warning light in Thaddeus's eyes, she sipped at the liquid. It was surprisingly pleasant.

'Mint tea,' Thaddeus told her as she settled back to enjoy her drink. 'There used to be quite an elaborate ceremony surrounding the drinking of mint tea,' he said, offering no more information.

'Well, go on—you obviously know it, so tell me,' she requested, amused by the deepening dimples in his cheeks.

'I thought you'd never ask,' he laughed, a deep, dangerous rumble that in the shadowy light of the tiny inn seemed quite seductive.

'The tea is made from fresh tea leaves, not dried like ours. It's packed into cold water with a great deal of sugar and heated till it boils. Then, at the right moment, more water, more sugar and mint are added. It's then passed from glass to pot several times. Finally the supreme moment is when the tea is poured.' He paused deliberately and Jenny nudged him in the ribs.

'Go *on*,' she complained, knowing that he was being deliberately provocative.

'Well, the idea then is for the host to pour the tea from the pot into the glasses from as high up as he can manage. The tea is supposed to stream down straight into the glass. The men are served first, more water added, the women served, more water added, then finally the elderly and children.'

'I see. Well, it sounds delightful, and tastes good too,' Jenny admitted.

'I don't suppose it happens much now. The women wouldn't like it,' he said, a trace of irony in his tone.

'What do you mean?' asked Jenny, knowing he was deliberately trying to goad her and trying hard not to rise to the bait.

'Well, equal rights—surely women would not be prepared to wait and drink after the men,' he said coolly, a malicious glint in his dark eyes.

'I'm sure I don't know,' Jenny replied. 'Their culture is so different from ours that I shouldn't like to comment.'

'But you can comment on *our* society, and women do expect equal rights?' he asked sharply, refusing to let the conversation drop despite the cunning reply Jenny had given.

'Yes, it is right that women are treated the same as men. It makes for a fairer society,' she countered. Thaddeus sighed audibly and Jenny wondered whether he was just being difficult to cause an argument.

'Come on, let's go. I'm sure there's plenty more to see,' she said with determination, ignoring his lack of interest. He seemed to want just to sit and talk, but Jenny sensed that an argument could soon develop. He shrugged his powerful shoulders lazily and a smile tugged at his sensuous mouth. Then he rose with lithe agility and pushed his arm through hers as he escorted her outside. Jenny tried to ignore the *frisson* of awareness that swept through her body at his touch.

'Let's go up to the lighthouse,' he said lightly, obviously fully refreshed after his drink. Jenny lifted her head to gaze upwards at the lighthouse that was perched on the top of the hill. The ascent was long and she was grateful for the firm, almost possessive grip Thaddeus's arm had taken of hers.

The view from the top justified the exhausting climb. Jenny's eyes swept over the panoramic view. The village seemed to cascade down the hill. The blue of the sea and sky matched the blue wooden trim and window-borders of the sugar-cube houses.

'Isn't it wonderful?' she breathed, turning to face Thaddeus, whose eyes were also fixed dreamily on the distant horizon. Jenny stared at his handsome profile, his lean, muscular face catching the sunlight, which softened his usually harsh features. Her heart quickened as he suddenly turned and looked at her and for one brief, almost glorious moment they were both trans-fixed, immobile as if caught in some magical spell. Thaddeus moved towards her as if drawn by some hidden magnet, and Jenny caught his movement and jumped slightly. She swallowed nervously as she stepped back, strangely aware of a danger, some raw and deeply sexual overtone that alarmed her.

Thaddeus noticed immediately the change and a wry smile teased his lips.

'If you've finished taking photos, let's go and see the craftsmen,' he said dismissively.

The cool breeze caught his hair, causing it to fall forward into his eyes. Without thinking Jenny reached out, her fingers becoming tangled in his heavy locks as she tried to stroke his hair back into place. She suddenly became aware of him, the touch of his skin and hair against her fingertips, and her stomach lurched. She stepped back, torn between fear and anger at herself. She had been so determined not to be affected by him, and yet inwardly her whole being seemed to crave to touch him. She dropped her hand to her side limply and moved back on to the busy streets; she felt safe in a crowd. They spent some time looking at the white and blue intricately made bird-cages that had made Sidi Bou Said famous.

'No matter how beautifully made, it's still a prison,' commented Thaddeus drily as he stroked the smooth cage with a deadly precision.

'Hardly a prison—the birds are well looked after, even loved.' Jenny laughed, trying to lighten the seriousness of his tone.

'Ah, love—we often cage what we love and by doing so destroy it,' he said wistfully and Jenny understood that he was no longer talking about the birds but about himself. She longed to question him, yet her mouth went dry before the words could be formed.

'Let's go,' he suddenly announced as if aware he had said too much. 'I fancy a swim.' And he caught her arm and led her back to the car.

CHAPTER SIX

JENNY took one last glance over her shoulder to fix the unique image in her mind before slipping into the car seat. Finally, after a long drive taken in silence, the road dipped and changed into a single-lane road. It curved dangerously sharply, and Thaddeus had to drop gear several times. Jenny's eyes darted nervously around and she tried to strain her neck to see if there was any oncoming traffic, but the road appeared completely deserted. Suddenly, just before the road twisted back up again, it shelved into a deserted beach. Jenny gave a gasp at the shimmering sea and stretch of perfect white sand in front of her.

'How on earth did you know about this place?' she said in surprise, her eyes wide in disbelief at the sheer beauty of the place.

'I had to do quite a bit of research before I came out here. I've been in correspondence with the local tourist office. They thought this might be ideal for filming the day scenes; we can hardly take over the tourist beaches.' He laughed as he stepped from the car. 'You change in here; the beach will be fine for me.' He laughed again, a deep, warm laugh that forced Jenny to smile.

She dug her toes into the hot white sand, enjoying the silky feel as it trailed between her toes. She could see Thaddeus some way off; he was looking out at the sea and she hurried to join him, aware that he had something on his mind. He was standing motionless, his blue eyes fixed upon some distant horizon, his thoughts miles away. She heard him sigh and her eyes darted to his.

'I like to be alone, away from everyone,' he said almost dreamily, and Jenny blushed at her intrusion and began to move away. He turned to look at her and caught the flush on her face.

'Don't—I didn't mean you. I was just thinking. My grandmother always lived with us, and her son, Uncle Josh. He had never married. Then, with Mum and Dad and five children, there never was a time for being on your own. Sometimes,' he said as he began a leisurely stroll down the beach, 'when I was little, I'd hide away in the hay-loft. I wouldn't come out even when they called me. I just wanted to be all on my own.' There was a note of regret in his voice.

'It must have been fun, though—lots of warmth and love,' she answered him, remembering how empty her own childhood had been.

'Yes, it was,' he recalled with a sigh. 'But I wasn't really a farmer's boy. I took after my mother; she wanted to be an actress. She loved the theatre, but she gave it all up for Dad. I was lucky I escaped. She made me; she wanted me to achieve what she couldn't with her life. It was such a waste,' he finished with a note of resentment on her behalf.

'I doubt your mother would agree with that. She may have loved the theatre, but she obviously loved your father more,' Jenny reasoned, a grey light of dawn beginning to filter through her mind. He saw marriage as a trap that prevented true fulfilment. He was determined not to get involved in case it affected his career.

'Probably not,' he agreed, 'but she missed out by getting married,' he countered.

Jenny said nothing—somehow she felt there was nothing to say—but she nodded in silent agreement, though she wasn't sure she did entirely agree. Thaddeus stooped to pick up a peace of driftwood from the beach. He scored a line in the fine sand as they strolled along.

The comfortable silence between them was only interrupted by the sound of the waves splashing gently against each other. It was a perfect setting, like paradise itself.

After a while, Thaddeus flopped on to the sand, stretching his long, lithe body up to the sun like a human sacrifice. He was already tanned, Jenny noticed as her eyes skimmed over his firm body, sending a thrill of anticipation through her. The memory of his kiss was still branded on her mind, and she knew her body would weaken if she allowed him to get too close.

'Aren't you going to sunbathe?' he asked, casting his long brown arm over his face to shield his eyes as he looked up at her.

'I need my beach-bag; I've got a towel and I'll have to put some protection on,' she said awkwardly, suddenly aware of the hungry look on his face and she tried to avoid it.

'OK,' he said, scrambling to his feet and catching her hand. The touch of his cool skin against hers was electrifying and she turned away rather than confront the intense look in his eyes. He clasped her hand gently as they raced back to the car. Jenny pulled her beach-bag from the back; Thaddeus opened the boot and pulled out a huge ice-box.

'It's not much, but we're bound to be hungry after a swim,' he said, putting the box down and spreading out a huge beach mat. 'Are you ready for a swim?' he asked, stretching out his hand for hers. Jenny faltered for a moment, aware of her own weakness, but to refuse would look rude. He grasped her hand tightly, his grip firm, and then a look of sudden confusion flashed in his eyes. Jenny understood immediately that he had felt the same jolt of desire as she had. They began to head for the gleaming waters and they ran in unison, splashing into the sea, in a flurry of foam. The water hit their bodies, cooling their hot skin, but within moments the water grew warmer as they waded in deeper. Jenny gave a cry of delight as a shoal of tiny silver fish swam in the crystal-clear water beneath her. She tried to catch one but her clumsy attempts made the fish scatter, only to re-assemble further away, always just a little out of reach. She slipped suddenly in the water and Thaddeus immediately reached out. His strong arm encircled her waist possessively and instantly Jenny tensed.

'Don't be afraid, Jennifer,' he whispered huskily. 'I'm not going to hurt you.' His voice was low and seductive. He moved closer till she could feel his warm breath on her face. 'You're a very attractive lady.' His voice was low-key and held a husky promise as he reached out and captured her face. Their eyes met and she could feel the steady thudding of his heart against her own increased tattoo. He looked down at the rise and fall of her ample breasts, then back to her face, searching for any sign of rejection.

Their bodies slid together, the warm waters pushing them into further intimacy. He pulled her ever closer, nibbling at the side of her neck. A series of delighted shock-waves rushed through her body, raising her temperature even higher. She found it difficult to think straight. She shouldn't let this happen, but with each passing moment her resistance weakened even more.

She groaned softly, unable and unwilling to fight him off. His soft lips moved slowly to her earlobe, gently catching the soft flesh between his teeth, and a *frisson* of delight ran the length of her spine. With deliberate insistence his tongue caressed her ear.

She had to stop him. The barriers she had erected with such care were dissolving under his masterful seduction. Each movement of his tongue increased her desire to respond.

'Don't,' she gasped, unable to suppress the natural urges she was feeling.

'Don't what?' he teased, as he moved his lips to her face. He traced the contours of her lips with the tip of his tongue, teasing the edge of her mouth apart till he gained entry. She felt dizzy, as if she was drunk, and she clung to his body, her arms automatically reaching out for him.

He lifted her easily from the water and carried to the beach, laying her down on the hot sand before covering her body with his. She could feel her breasts swelling against the hardness of his chest. His hands slid up from her waist to her ribs, then higher still to the thin swimsuit straps. Her skin was growing hotter under his expert touch and his fingers pushed away her straps with ease. His hand enveloped her breast, his thumb flicking over her taut nipple till he heard her groan with pleasure.

His kisses were increasing in strength, and Jenny knew she had to put a stop to what they were doing. Yet each stroke of his fingers seemed to increase her need for him. She wanted to pull away but seemed to be too weak to move, her own body, intent on betrayal, seeming to mould to his masculine contours. She could feel the wild beating of her heart against his chest like a trapped bird wanting its freedom.

'Jennifer,' he moaned, the urgency in his voice alarming her. She shuddered as his lips found the hardness of her swollen nipples, her body arching against his. She wasn't ready for this—she was suddenly aware of his state of arousal and it frightened her. Her body seemed to be crying out for satisfaction but her mind was racing with denials.

She fought hard to resist and Thaddeus seemed to sense her inner struggle. He moved away a little and she looked at him, her eyes wide with surprise. His breathing was equally ragged, and the look in his eyes was still slumberous and inviting.

'No,' she mumbled, her voice barely audible above the sound of the waves. 'I can't.' She lowered her head as if ashamed of the admission.

Thaddeus said nothing for what seemed an eternity, and Jenny waited, her heart beating rapidly, her mind confused by what had just taken place. She wondered how he would react to her refusal. She wasn't sure, and guilt washed over her like the waves of the sea as she realised how willing she had been. The thought was terrifying.

'I'm so sorry,' she said, shaking her head, trying to break the silence between them. She kept her head lowered, her eyes hooded so she could not see his expression.

His fingers pressed the underneath of her chin, his touch searing her body with the heat. He pulled her face upwards and she was surprised by the tender look on his face. A frown furrowed his brow as he gazed into her eyes.

'Sorry?' he echoed. 'There's no need. There will be other times,' he whispered, capturing her lips again and kissing her gently.

Jenny heard alarm bells ring in her head. His threatening words could indeed become a reality if she was not careful. She was not prepared to become yet another one of his conquests.

She jumped to her feet, pulling the straps back up on to her shoulders. Her body was stiff with anger. She saw a flicker of amusement in his eyes that infuriated her.

'Mr Clarke, I'm here to do a job,' she emphasised carefully. 'I am not, however, prepared to become yet another one of your perks. I would appreciate it if there was not a repetition of your behaviour.' Frostily she turned away to go back to the car.

He was on his feet in seconds with a speed that took her by surprise. He caught her deftly by the wrist and spun her round. The look of warmth had evaporated from his face and his jaw had tensed in a firm, angry mask.

'It takes two to tango, and you were a more than willing partner,' he growled.

Jenny coloured immediately as the truth of his words stung her. She tried to pull away, but his grip remained firm and her struggle was in vain.

'It's going to happen sooner or later, and I'm willing to wait,' he concluded.

His faith in himself infuriated Jenny and her eyes flashed with unconcealed rage. She tossed her head back, viewing him with as much disdain as she could muster under his searing gaze.

'Well, you're in for a long wait,' she snapped at him.

'Am I?' he laughed, lightly brushing his lips across her cheek. Jenny closed her eyes as her pulses leapt. He drew back immediately. 'See,' he mocked as he released her arm.

Jenny was unable to think of anything suitable to say. Her body seemed to be acting without her consent. She gave him what she hoped was a look of disgust and marched away with as much dignity as she possessed. She could hear his quiet laughter ringing in her ears as she struggled quickly back into her clothes.

The drive back to the hotel was conducted in silence, and Jenny forced herself to stare out of the side-window. She was unable to stand the look of amusement that gleamed in Thaddeus's eyes and the mocking grin that seemed to tug relentlessly at his sensuous mouth. The moment the car stopped Jenny was out and racing for the sanctuary of her hotel room. Thaddeus's voice carried in the still heat of the day as he said, 'Dinner tonight at eight.'

Jenny spun around, but her refusal died on her lips when he added, 'Bring your camera. I think it will make an excellent location.'

Jenny nodded dumbly in response, feeling oddly deflated. She had deluded herself again, imagining he was making a personal invitation. That was so foolish—had she not just rebuffed his advances? Yet somehow deep inside she felt disappointed.

At five to eight that evening Jenny knocked on Thaddeus's door and called his name, but there was no answer. She opened the door tentatively and scanned the room. He was asleep, stretched out on top of the bed wearing only a pair of boxer shorts, and Jenny's pulse leapt when she saw him. She felt a rush of colour to her face as she inwardly reacted to his form.

The open window caressed his body with a cool breeze, the curtain casting a changing pattern across his bare chest. She crossed the room towards him, trying to suffocate the turmoil she felt inside. Even in his sleep there was no hiding the fact he was a formidable man.

She drew closer before realising that he was already awake. He must have been watching her, and the thought unnerved her still further. Jenny felt her confidence drain away. He was still sleepy, and his eyes were dark with a slumberous warmth that held a wicked invitation. His mouth relaxed into a sensuously moulded smile. Jenny felt a tell-tale ache stir deep within her, her body betraying her true feelings.

Logic was all forgotten as she felt her body responding to him despite the frantic messages she was sending to her brain. He moved slowly towards her like a panther sure of his prey. Jenny's eyes dilated slightly as he approached her, yet she seemed unable to move. Trapped by his hypnotic gaze, she felt herself shiver involuntarily, though it was still warm. There was a naked hunger in his expression as his finger firmly but gently traced the outline of her lips. Jenny gasped at his touch, a burning sensation rushing through her body.

His head came slowly down and Jenny closed her eyes as his lips scorched hers. He awoke in her an exquisite longing, struck deep down in the core of her being. Her whole body was alive, tingling with anticipation, and her defences were crumbling as his lips melted against hers. She longed to reach out to hold him, to feel his hard chest against hers. Yet she stiffened, still unsure, and he drew back, aware of her action. For a moment he looked angry, then he gave a slow, wry smile.

'Wait for me in the bar,' he instructed her coolly and Jenny, amazed at his composure, just nodded dumbly by way of response. She hurried away and sat alone in the bar, her mind in turmoil, ideas racing around in her head till she was forced to admit that, despite the defensive walls she had erected around herself, Thaddeus Clarke had broken them down. She loved him, despite all her determination not to be so foolish. She had fallen in love with him. She felt such a fool; the man was the devil incarnate and made no pretence about it. He wanted her sexually, but that was all, she thought miserably, shaking her head. She could not afford to let him know her true feelings; she had to keep them secret; she would hate him to realise. No doubt if he did he would use the knowledge to his own advantage. Yet the very thought of him made her weaken. She was frightened by the uncontrollable way her own body reacted to him.

The bar was deserted, and Jenny sat in the corner, her mind a riot of confusion as she tried in vain to suffocate the havoc of feelings he arose in her. The moment he appeared she felt her stomach turn over. He was so handsome; he had already managed to catch the sun and his face held a warm tan. He was dressed casually, in a plain white short-sleeved shirt and a pair of plain grey trousers.

'We're not eating here,' he told her as she moved towards the restaurant. 'I'm taking you somewhere special,' he added mysteriously. Jenny smiled at him, though she found it increasingly difficult to represent a cool, calm façade when inwardly she was a vortex of

emotions. Jenny was resolute, however, that she would
not allow her inner turmoil to be revealed.

It was a short walk before they reached their desti-
nation. Jenny made polite small talk the whole time,
even though she was painfully aware of every movement
he made. She was grateful when they finally arrived at
the restaurant. She wanted the solid table between them,
as a barrier, a defence against his aura of sexuality. She
was disappointed: the interior of the restaurant bore no
resemblance to its normal exterior. A large canopy filled
the centre of the room, like a huge red tent. It was
trimmed with tassels of golden silken thread and heavy
multi-patterned rugs filled the floor. Numerous cushions
of varying sizes and shapes were thrown in a haphazard
way and Jenny panicked as she realised that the place
was empty apart from them.

'We're eating here?' she gasped; it reminded her of
the *Arabian Nights*, and a vivid image of Thaddeus as
a sheikh flashed through her mind. He nodded as he
collapsed on to some cushions with casual aplomb and
suggested she do the same. Jenny hesitated a moment
too long, and Thaddeus snatched her hand and pulled
her down beside him. She fell on to the cushions in an
untidy heap as a *frisson* of delight coursed through her
body at his touch.

The meal was like a banquet, an assortment of different foods. A tangy plate of *méchouia* was served first.
It was a dish made of tomatoes, hot peppers, onions,
salted lemons and capers all cooked in olive oil then
sprinkled with tuna fish and hard-boiled eggs. Each dish
complemented the next and Jenny ate for once totally
unconscious of what she was doing. Thaddeus lay at the

side of her, his head propped up by his arm, and watched her with increasing delight.

'You have eaten well this evening,' he noted, and Jenny nodded in full agreement. Being in love had certainly given her an appetite.

'So have you,' she laughed back, always amazed at how much he ate.

'But not all my appetites are satisfied,' he said quietly, his voice low, and a slow, deliberate smile creased his face. He fixed his eyes on Jenny and she felt compelled to look at him, though she knew it was fatal. She took a clementine from the small brass dish he offered her and smiled her thanks. She peeled the fruit with care before sinking her pearl-white teeth into its soft flesh, fully aware that he was watching her every move.

'Jennifer,' he whispered softly in her ear; there was an unspoken invitation in his voice that her body longed to answer. She melted at the side of him, allowing her body to mould against his chest and he groaned as she did.

'Let's go the beach,' he said suddenly, stiffening and almost pushing her away. Jenny felt a sudden stab of regret. Had she made her feelings so obvious? Her legs seemed leaden and her feet dragged as she walked beside him. She became aware of the clear midnight sky and full silver moon. It seemed to mock her romantic notions, and her heart sunk even further. The whole situation was so futile and yet Jenny was all too aware of the powerful sexual attraction between them.

She pulled her sandals off once they reached the beach. The sand was cool and soft and her feet sank with ease into the silvery white sand. She could hear the sound of the sea, far away, splashing relentlessly against a hidden shoreline. Thaddeus wrapped his arm around her waist, drawing her closer, and she looked up. He was gazing out into the blackness of the night. The moonlight shone in his hair, catching its dark blue highlights and softening his strong features. He looked down and smiled when he saw her.

'On our farm it was always bustling, full of life, and yet you live in the country and it seemed so quiet, empty. I liked that, the peace—but don't you ever want to share it?' he questioned gently, sensing her loneliness. Jenny tensed automatically. She had lived alone for so long, shut herself away from the pain of involvement, and yet here was someone who made her long to change her sterile existence.

'Not yet,' she answered untruthfully, turning away so he could not see the pain in her eyes. He was far too perceptive and she had told him enough already.

'I'm like that. When I first left home I was really homesick. I missed everyone, I felt so alone, but after a while I realised how much I enjoyed being on my own. For the first time in my life I could take a bath without joining a queue, eat what I wanted when I wanted. I was free.'

'So you never see yourself getting involved, making a lasting commitment to someone?' she asked, trying to sound indifferent, though her heart was plummeting inside her. Thaddeus shrugged his strong shoulders and a low rumble of laughter bubbled up inside him.

'You're beautiful,' he whispered, his warm breath caressing her cheek, and she blushed at the compliment. Yet she was still aware that he had avoided answering her question. He stroked the side of her face with the back of his hand and pulled her into his arms. She wanted him to kiss her, wanted to feel his hot lips claiming hers, and she opened her mouth as she raised her head. The kiss was magical, tormentingly slow, yet it held an urgency to which she instinctively responded. She held him tighter, her fingers pulling at him till her soft swelling breasts were hard against his chest. The kissing was becoming more heated and Jenny groaned as she moved rhythmically against him, her body demanding satisfaction.

'Jennifer,' he pleaded as he drew back, 'you don't know what you're doing. I'm human for God's sake.'

'I do know,' she answered confidently, fixing her eyes on him. She could deny herself no longer. She wanted him despite the fact he would not be willing to make a long-term commitment. Jenny knew she was, but if she did not respond she might regret it for the rest of her life. He smiled as he saw the wondrous light of love in her eyes and they walked back along the beach to their hotel in mutual silence, as if to speak would break the strong bond that had been forged between them. The desire of the last few days had built up inside her and her body ached with it.

In her room Thaddeus put the bedside lamp on, its pink shade casting a rosy glow over the pristine white sheets. He sank on to the bed, raising his hand in invitation. Jenny looked into his eyes. They had darkened to the darkest black and she felt an icy trickling down her spine.

'Jen.' His voice was husky and deep, heavy with the tension and emotion they were both feeling. Jenny stood transfixed; she knew there was no turning back, that this was the last time he was going to ask. She stared at him, taking in his handsome face, the dark wing of his hair, his mouth so perfect that need for him soared within her, higher than an eagle on a mountain range. She moved closer, her tongue travelling over her dry mouth with a slow deliberation.

He drew her down and kissed her. A kiss that finally shattered any last doubts, it was hard and demanding, full of the pent-up frustrations of the last few days. There was a desperation in her own response that only increased his desire for her and she moaned with abandon as his mouth covered hers.

In the darkness of Jenny's bed they sought each other, their mouths moving hungrily over each other's faces with unbridled passion. She was responding with all the ardency of her generous nature. His immense frame covered her, enveloping her with the hard strength of his body. Their clothes were discarded as they helped each other to undress, eager to feel each other's naked skin. She shuddered as his warm bare flesh touched hers and she tentatively stroked her hand across his back as he murmured her name. She was lost in a dream, her body immersed in the waters of overwhelming desire as he moved his strong body over hers. She tried to focus on him to give herself some direction as she lost herself in a world of growing sensations. His eyes were too dark, like black orbs, piercing into her very being with their glittering shafts. She moaned as the mat of rough hairs that covered his chest prickled against her swelling breasts, which ached, craving for his touch. She pushed herself up against him, enjoying her new sense of power as he tensed at her touch. She moaned softly as his hands wrapped around her waist, drawing her up to him and kissing her lips with a raw passion that she had never dreamed possible.

'God, you're so beautiful,' his smoky voice drawled as his hot lips trailed down her neck towards her taut nipples. Jenny shivered with anticipation as his lips kissed her ample breast, at first tenderly, but then with an urgency that alerted her to his needs. His teeth sank into her soft flesh, soft, biting kisses that made her heart quicken to an alarming speed. His fingers circled her breast and he stroked his thumb across her nipple till she cried out, sinking her nails into his hard back.

Her body was alive, vibrant and tingling; she ached for fulfilment and arched herself against him. She could sense his smile, feel the warmth of it as he refused to comply to her wishes. His hands stroked the length of her body, and it gleamed with the glow of pinky light. She could hear his muffled voice murmuring words of appreciation as he caressed her skin, and her heart soared. The knowledge that she had a beautiful body only increased her own desire. He skilfully parted her legs with a gentle but firm stroke and Jenny momentarily froze at the intimacy of his touch. She felt oddly vulnerable, almost frightened, but her fears were soon overcome with an exquisite, almost unbearable pleasure. She clung to his shoulders, pulling him down towards her, unable to cope with the dizzy heights to which she had ascended. His hand supported her spine and her whole body throbbed with desire, both of them freely giving themselves, seeking to give each other pleasure till they soared like birds of the air. They were lost to the world; the only reality they knew was each other as their bodies fused together and they achieved the oneness they sought.

Jenny cried out his name as her body shook uncontrollably, and he held her tightly in his arms, whispering gentle words of love to her. Exhausted, they lay in each other's arms, their bodies still intertwined. Jenny rested in the crook of his arm, her head weighing heavily on his chest. She fell into a deep and wondrous sleep, safe and confident in his love for her.

CHAPTER SEVEN

WHEN Jenny awoke in the morning, she was still feeling as if she was floating on air. She turned and watched Thaddeus dressing, pulling on his trousers over his strong legs, his T-shirt falling against his muscular chest. She watched him with interest, a possessive gleam in her eyes as she made a full inventory of him.

'Good morning,' she said at last.

He stiffened at the sound of her voice and raised his dark head to look at her. 'Why didn't you tell me?' he demanded, his voice hoarse, full of emotion.

'Tell you?' she echoed, not understanding him but sensing something was wrong—something had spoiled everything.

'I didn't realise you were a virgin...' He paused, his cheeks taking on a reddish hue that vanished as quickly as it had appeared. 'I just presumed—well, you and Pablo...' He couldn't continue and Jenny knew why. He felt guilty; there was no love there, only sexual satisfaction.

'Forget it. It was no big deal,' she lied, trying to keep the pain from her voice.

'Jennifer, I want to talk to you...' he began, but she stiffened immediately. She knew what he was about to say, how it had all been a mistake, and she hated herself for falling for his charm.

'I'd rather not talk about it,' she blurted out, already leaping from the bed and darting for the bathroom. A sick feeling came over her: she had felt she had found real love; she had fooled herself once again. He was as lithe and as quick as usual, and caught her arm as she tried to flee from him. He pulled her against him in an oddly protective way and she swallowed the desire to weaken at his touch.

'We *must* talk, Jennifer.'

'No!' she almost shouted as she became rigid in his arms. She didn't want to hear it; he had never made any pretence of the type of man he was.

Commitment was the last thing he wanted, and Jenny wanted him to believe that she agreed.

She didn't regret their lovemaking; she knew it had been inevitable. The strength of attraction between them was undeniable; if she had been silly enough to fall for him, that was her problem, and she certainly didn't want his sympathy now.

'Leave me alone,' she snapped. 'I can do without your pity.' The bitterness in her voice was stinging and sharp.

He jerked her head up swiftly, knocking her teeth together with a click. He stared at her, his eyes like shards of blue diamonds and equally hard. She closed her eyes to block out his harsh features but he grasped her hair tightly and rasped. 'Look at me, damn you.' His voice was cold and furious, and Jenny's eyes shot open, trapped by his steely gaze.

'Pity? Pity!' he spat at her through his clenched teeth. 'Yes, I do pity you, but not for the reasons you think,' he barked as he thrust her aside. He stopped at the door and cast her look of sheer fury. 'Don't forget the rest of the crew start arriving this afternoon. Keep well out of my way till then and you should be safe,' he sneered, as he slammed the door behind him.

Jenny did just that, even ordering breakfast and lunch be sent up to her room. At one o'clock she knew she could delay no longer and she went downstairs in her most official manner. She dressed for the part, choosing a pair of white cotton trousers and a simple round-necked blouse. She carried her clipboard in front of her like a shield and wore dark glasses to hide the redness of her eyes. She didn't want him to know she had been crying.

Jenny froze at the foot of the stairs; there was no mistaking Thaddeus even when he had his back to her—but she couldn't believe her ears. The clear, strong French accent carried over the foyer and he spoke with perfect ease and fluency. Yet another deception—he had sworn her services would be essential as he had no knowledge of the language.

Jenny felt a bubble of anger swelling up inside her. How could she have allowed herself to be so easily fooled? Her features distorted into a grimace with annoyance and that moment he turned and faced her. For a fleeting moment she thought she saw a look of regret, but it was soon replaced with a frozen look of anger.

'You can sort out the rest of the crew's rooms,' he said in a clipped tone, ignoring the look of wrath on her face. Jenny felt her chest tighten with emotion as she tried to comprehend his deceit. What advantage was it to Thaddeus? She couldn't understand; her mind was a complete blank.

'Wait!' she called after him as he started to move away. He spun round, his face suddenly clouding with anger when she asked, 'When is my replacement arriving?' Her voice was clear and direct and carried across the foyer. She knew she had to sound confident and determined. He viewed her, his face grim, totally lacking in the love

she had so readily seen the night before. Jenny's heart
sank as she realised how foolish she had been.

'Soon,' he answered briefly, and marched away before
she had the chance to question him further. She watched
him walk away, still suspicious that there seemed to be
no mention of a replacement on her papers. The rest of
the crew had all arrived together, and it was only a matter
of days before the actors themselves would be here—and
she was determined to be gone by then. A niggling doubt
began to fester at the back of her mind which increased
her anxiety. She was no longer sure that Thaddeus had
arranged for a replacement PA.

'Mr Clarke, if you have a moment.' She interrupted
his meal. She had no desire to have this conversation
with an audience watching. She was already aware that
gossip was rife and she didn't want to add any more fuel
to the fire.

He glanced up, acknowledging her presence with a
nod, and directed her to sit down. She ignored his offer
and stiffened herself for battle. She didn't want to sit
with him, to recall past meals and the intimacy they had
known.

'I'd rather stand—it won't take long. I just want to
know exactly when my replacement is arriving,' she told
him curtly, trying to keep the tremor from her voice. He
carried on eating for a moment as if considering how to
answer her, then he looked up.

'There is no replacement. I would have thought you
would have worked that out by now,' he said evenly. He
continued to eat as if she wasn't even there.

Jenny had always kept her emotions under strict
control; for years she had denied herself the simple
luxury of being human. She was always frightened of

letting go, afraid of the consequences for her. She had survived through all her problems, coped and won. Now she was ready to give full rein to her emotions—including temper. Thaddeus's arrogant, unfeeling and deceitful attitude triggered off all the unspent anger of many years. She stared at him for a moment as her temper continued to rise, welling up inside her like the boiling lava in a volcano. Then, in one swift movement, she seized up his wine glass and threw the wine across his face.

'You bastard,' she spat at him, her voice low and full of hatred, her eyes piercing and sharp.

Thaddeus rose to his feet in one fluid movement, the chair he was sitting on falling to the ground with the force of his body. He snatched up his napkin, wiping the red wine from his face. Each movement was exacted with slow deliberation for greatest impact, and Jenny shrank back when she saw the menace in his eyes. His face was lean and hard; no glimmer of softness in his features.

'Out!' he growled at her before his lips snapped shut again into a grim, angry line.

Jenny faltered for a moment, an apology forming on her lips as she contemplated the consequences of her action. His eyes narrowed still further at what he interpreted as refusal, and his voice took on an even more threatening tone as he repeated in a hoarse whisper, 'Get out of here, Miss Collins.'

Jenny turned and fled. Her heart was thudding painfully against her chest and her breathing was rapid and shallow. She looked round the foyer in desperation; she wanted to hide, to wait till he had cooled down before she faced him. Her room was out of the question—that would be the first place he would look.

She started for the main entrance but she was too late. Thaddeus's voice cut across the foyer with unmistakable anger.

'Where do you think you're going?' he roared, unbothered by the other guests mingling around.

Jenny paid no heed except to increase her pace slightly—to start to run would reveal her fear and draw even more attention to her. Thaddeus caught her arm in a tight punitive grip and he spun her round.

'Not so fast,' he drawled dangerously as she tried to pull away, forcing her to land on his hard chest, but she sought no comfort there, not this time. 'We have some serious talking to do,' he warned her quietly.

Jenny glared at him, her fists becoming tight angry balls. 'Talking! Can you manage that? All I've ever had from you is lies,' she accused him angrily.

A cruel smile curved his lips. 'Is that a fact?' he sneered, his voice so low and angry that her blood ran cold. 'Well, believe this—you come straight up to my room now or I'll carry you.' He watched her, his body stiff and threatening.

'You wouldn't...' she began.

'Yes?' he enquired, his eyebrows raised in mockery, a slow smile tugging at his lips as he held her.

She lowered her head in defeat, her mouth tight and angry. She felt her heart beat out a slow, desperate thud as she walked slowly to the lift. They stood together silently as the lift doors closed, and for one frantic moment Jenny thought she would dive between the closing doors, but as if he had anticipated her reaction he clasped her hand in his.

Jenny's nerves tightened with every floor, and she cast a nervous glance at his face. There remained a few telltale spots of wine, and his shirt was ruined with a dramatic splash across the front. She had never seen him so distant, so in control, and it only increased her tension.

'Go on,' he told her brusquely, opening the door to his room and following close behind. 'Sit,' he barked as if speaking to a dog as he marched past her and into the bathroom. Jenny obeyed willingly, for she felt her legs would give beneath her at any moment.

She heard the splashing of water and he came back into the room, towelling himself dry. She watched him warily as he opened a drawer and pulled out a fresh shirt. He then made his way across the room, each stride calculated with a purposefulness that unnerved her still further. She looked up sharply as he approached and frowned.

'I'm sorry,' she blurted out, unable to accept the silence any longer. It was fraying her nerves.

'Who's lying now?' he reminded her softly, toying with a loose strand of her hair. She felt a *frisson* of excitement—there was a sensuality and danger in his action which she found disturbingly attractive.

'I think you owe me some sort of compensation, for my shirt—don't you, Jennifer?' he said huskily, drawing closer till she caught the scent of his aftershave. Jenny pushed him away and stood up, her face red with anger and her eyes as bright as day.

'Get lost. The only compensation you'll get from me is if you send me the laundry bill,' she said angrily, hating the way her body was so ready to weaken. 'I came here to set up the locations. I've done that. Now I want to go back,' she said emphatically.

He rose in front of her, pushing her back into her seat and towering over it. 'Well, tough, because you're here and you're not going anywhere till the job's finished,' he informed her crisply, his dark face brooding.

She hated him, the casual way he disregarded her feelings. She was determined not to stay; she couldn't stand it. Thaddeus, Pablo and Margaret—the situation was hopeless. She was determined to make him understand.

'I have to go,' she snapped, her expression angry as she looked at him.

'Why?' he asked, the softness in his tone strangely at odds with the unrelenting look on his face. 'Is Pablo still that important to you?' he asked suddenly, venomously.

Jenny sucked in her breath, glaring at him with hatred. 'That's not the issue here,' she protested between her teeth, amazed by the insult after last night's events. Was his opinion of her that low? Her eyes were wide and sparkling, a bright, angry amber against the pale curve of her face. Thaddeus gave a low laugh of mockery.

'I think it is: you still love him, don't you?'

Jenny's cheeks flushed. 'It's none of your business,' she countered, hearing the shallowness of her own words when they had shared so much.

'It's my damn business if it interferes with your job,' he reminded her forcefully.

She jerked her head back as if she had been struck. That was the final insult—the knowledge that their love-making had meant nothing. Her face was bitterly angry as she snapped, 'Well, stuff the job. I resign.'

A cold smile of derision crept across his face and he viewed her with mild amusement.

'Fine. You can work your notice while on this job.' He laughed cruelly.

Jenny stared at him in hostile silence, feeling her temper rise like a huge wild flame inside her. 'No, I refuse,' she snapped in a low, angry voice. 'You can't make me.'

'It's in your contract,' he reminded her with a steely edge in his voice. 'The choice is yours.' He shrugged his powerful shoulders, the victory already claimed. Jenny gritted her teeth in anger, her fists clenching tightly at her sides. 'Well?' he drawled triumphantly, watching her actions closely.

Jenny glared at him, defeat and frustration coiling up inside her till she wanted to scream. She rose from the chair with as much dignity as she could muster and walked slowly from the room, determined not to give him the satisfaction of seeing how angry she was.

As she opened the door he called, 'Jennifer?'

She turned to face him. 'Yes?' she replied frostily.

'I'll send you the laundry bill for the shirt,' he reminded her. Then he smiled, his sensuous mouth widening to reveal his perfect white teeth. His smile grew even further at her furious expression till his dimples showed.

'Do that, Mr Clarke,' she retorted, slamming the door and trying to shut out the visual impact of his smile. She stormed back to her room, tears of frustration and pain welling up in her eyes.

'Damn! Damn! Damn the man,' she muttered to herself angrily as she paced the room. She was trapped; even if she did resign, she would still have to complete this job first. Jenny sank on to the bed in despair, rubbing her forehead as she tried to reason out a solution, but after two hours she was no further on. The sudden rap on her door made her jump and she was on her feet immediately.

'Come in,' she called, hoping her eyes did not betray the tears she had been shedding. Thaddeus marched in, his face animated and his beaming smile devastating.

'Dinner tonight, in the hotel at eight o'clock,' he said brusquely, then added in a gentler tone, 'We shall have a guest, so look your best.'

Jenny stared at him, nonplussed. Surely he couldn't expect her to carry on as if nothing had happened?

'You're joking. I can't possibly——' she began, but Thaddeus cut in at once, a flash of annoyance cutting across his face.

'You can and you will. This dinner is very important. Be there.' There was a warning threat in his quiet tone, and Jenny shivered as he strode out of the room, slamming the door noisily behind him. She then fell on the bed and muffled a scream of total frustration into the pillow as her hands thumped the bed mercilessly.

Jenny turned slowly in front of the full-length mirror, checking with care how she looked. She gave a smile of satisfaction as she ran her hand over her dress to smooth out any tiny wrinkles. It was a simple dress, cream silk with a drop waist and pleated skirt. It complemented her hair colour and she had applied a little make-up that drew attention to the clear beauty of her hazel eyes. She left her hair loose, falling about her shoulders in gentle waves of gold. She fastened a slim gold chain around her neck and picked up her evening bag, confident that she looked good.

It was strange to be going to dinner with Thaddeus, thought Jenny as she made her way downstairs. It was slightly ironic in the circumstances. She sighed. Her heart still raced the moment she saw him.

He made his way purposefully towards her, taking her hand with gentle possession. Jenny's pulses leapt at his touch, a flood of colour filling her face. She lowered her eyes quickly, but not before she caught the look of desire in his. She trembled slightly, suddenly aware of her own feelings. Thaddeus escorted her to the table, drawing out her chair with customary ease before sitting on the opposite side of the table. Jenny's eyes darted round the table uncomfortably.

'Just one other guest?' she asked, puzzled at why she had been invited. It certainly was not normal procedure, and she instinctively knew Thaddeus was up to something.

'Yes,' he replied, non-committal, as he ordered them both an aperitif.

Jenny watched him thoughtfully as she sipped her martini. He seemed on edge, not his usual self, and she wondered who could cause such a reaction.

Suddenly he sprang to his feet, his eyes gleaming with triumph. A buzz of conversation rippled around the room, but Jenny was unable to see who was the cause of it. She craned her neck and her eyes widened in disbelief. Margaret Miller had swept into the dining hall. No wonder people were talking. A series of flashing camera-lights flickered and she paused to allow photographs.

Jenny frowned, watching Margaret nodding regally to her fans, a fixed false smile on her perfectly made-up face. She couldn't believe it; then, as she saw Thaddeus approach Margaret, a cold dread of realisation hit her. Her eyes flew to Thaddeus, then to Margaret, and her stomach somersaulted. She felt sick and beads of perspiration broke out on her back. She swallowed nervously.

Margaret looked as stunning as ever. Her mass of red hair was piled on top of her head in an elaborate style and her dress was so closely fitted that Jenny puzzled to know how she had got into it. It fitted like a second skin, giving emphasis to every dip and curve.

Jenny watched her in quiet fascination as she approached. She knew her heart was racing and automatically began to stand as she drew nearer. She could feel Thaddeus's eyes upon her and she darted a covert glance at him. There was a flash in his eyes that warned her to behave and she felt a hysterical bubble of laughter inside her. It was only for a split second, but it seemed like an eternity that Margaret and she faced each other. Then Margaret opened her arms wide, tears of affection springing to her eyes.

Jenny wasted no time; she fell into her arms, hugging her desperately. For a moment they were unaware of Thaddeus's reaction, but as they drew apart they were both amused by the stunned look on his face. Margaret dabbed at her eyes and wrapped a protective arm around Jenny.

'You look marvellous, Sis,' she enthused, sitting next to her, oblivious to everyone else.

'And you,' replied Jenny, suddenly relaxing. She was glad Margaret was here. It was time to make amends, to heal rifts.

'Margaret Miller is your sister?' Thaddeus broke in, unable to keep the surprise from his voice. Jenny nodded briefly, remembering all she had told Thaddeus. 'Why all the secrecy?' he asked, puzzled, and Jenny and Margaret laughed in unison, catching each other's hand and holding on to one another. Margaret began to explain.

'There are lots of reasons. Jenny wanted to make her own career on her own. She didn't want to get jobs merely because the director could use her as a stepping-stone to me. Secondly——' began Margaret, but Jenny cut in, feeling it was all her fault,

'The other reason is that we parted last time on less than friendly terms.' Her eyes darted to Margaret anxiously, but there was no condemnation in her eyes.

'That's why I insisted Jenny Collins be on this job. I was determined we should get back together. Was it very difficult to persuade her?' Margaret asked, unaware of the hurt, angry look Jenny flashed at Thaddeus. Had he told her the real reason for his insistence, she would have come. Instead he'd been deceitful. Her eyes narrowed with distaste as she viewed him, but he met her hostile look with one of his own.

'You should have asked me yourself,' Jenny said to Margaret wistfully. 'It would have saved a lot of trouble,' she added meaningfully.

'That's all in the past now. Let's just forget it,' her sister reassured Jenny, who smiled back warmly, her heart spinning. 'You look well, very well, and there's a sparkle in your eyes,' she teased. 'Who is he?' she continued as Jenny's face flooded with colour.

'No one!' Jenny snapped, aware of the sharpness in her tone and the irritated glance she received from Thaddeus.

'You're not still...' began Margaret, an anxious tone in her voice and her eyes troubled.

'No, no, of course not—I was over him a long time ago,' Jenny cut in, reassuring her sister and unaware of the sigh of relief that escaped the older woman's lips.

'I'm glad about that, Jen, because he came with me tonight. I didn't want to bring him in just in case...'

'Paul is here?' gasped Jenny, her heart lurching and her stomach sinking.

'Pablo,' corrected Margaret softly. 'We flew in together today. He's still not sure about this film and I told him I was having dinner tonight with the director. It seemed an ideal opportunity to talk any doubts through,' she explained briefly. Before Jenny could answer, Thaddeus had intervened with a speed that left Jenny speechless.

'Of course—let's get it all thrashed out here and now so filming can begin,' he said enthusiastically, and Margaret gave a smile of gratitude as she left the table. Jenny's eyes flew to Thaddeus, sparks of anger flying from them.

'How dare you?' she spat at him. 'You used me on this job, didn't you?' she demanded, the hurt inside cutting her deeply. 'The only way Margaret would agree was if I was here, right?' she snapped, but didn't wait for a reply to her question. She already knew the answer. 'And now,' she continued, her disbelief echoing in her tone, 'you invite Paul to join us!'

Thaddeus caught her wrist in a tight grip, his voice low as he hissed, 'Keep your damn voice down. Yes, you're right; Margaret would only agree to do the job if you were here. So I made sure you were. It was deceitful, but so were you. You seemed to conveniently forget she was your sister,' he bit out at her, the brooding dark storm swirling in his eyes. Jenny tried to pull away but his grip tightened further and she was forced to remain seated.

'Let go. I can't face him.' There was a plea in her voice that he remained immune to.

'You're over him, remember?' he spat, the venom in his voice surprising her. She looked at him and met his hostile gaze. The intensity startled her and she quickly looked away, unable to hold it for more than a few seconds.

'Do you still care for him?' he demanded.

Jenny stiffened sharply, suddenly filled with unaccountable alarm. Unease stirred inside her and her heart began to beat a slow, heavy rhythm. A shrill voice rang in her head. Did she care? She shut her eyes to block out the thought.

'Do you?' Thaddeus's voice was low and hoarse, but Jenny didn't answer, and as she opened her eyes she saw Pablo approaching. Her stricken face conveyed her feelings as she felt her body freeze. Pablo walked with the casual, easy stride he was famous for. He was even more handsome than she remembered. The wealth which he had acquired with his success only added to his attractiveness. Instead of the torn, faded jeans he used to wear, and scuffed trainers, he now wore designer suits and soft Italian leather shoes. His skin was permanently tanned, a deep golden shade that enhanced the chocolate-brown warmth of his eyes. Jenny stared, her eyes wide as she took it all in.

'Well, if you're immune to him,' mocked Thaddeus in a drawling voice, 'then you're the only woman in the room.'

A mocking smile curled his lips as Jenny's eyes flashed to his face. She wanted to slap the smile off his face.

'Here's Pablo,' introduced Margaret.

But Jenny wasn't even listening. She was staring at Thaddeus Clarke with intense hatred.

CHAPTER EIGHT

THERE was a little silence. Then Thaddeus said in the friendliest of manners, 'Delighted, Mr Tagore,' extending his arm and shaking Pablo's hand. Pablo responded with a charming smile and his eyes flicked over to Jenny. She took a steadying breath and her face broke into a smile.

'Hello,' she managed to say, then raised her glass and took a great gulp of martini to steady her nerves. Thaddeus watched her with a frown and she caught a glint of anger in his eyes. Margaret sat back down next to Jenny and gave her hand a comforting squeeze, a look of sympathy on her face. Jenny wanted to protest; it was not Pablo who was concerning her, it was Thaddeus Clarke.

The conversation soon began in earnest about the production and Jenny was grateful to take a back seat. She sat eating her food with uninterest, toying with the delicate sauce that surrounded the perfectly cooked fish. Suddenly she became aware of Thaddeus's contemptuous look—his eyes seared her soul with their intensity. Jenny shivered uncomfortably.

'Jenny, you're looking very lovely.' Pablo's smooth voice grated on Jenny's stretched nerves. She swallowed nervously, more aware of Thaddeus's grim expression than the smile on Pablo's face. 'Will you have a sweet?' Pablo offered generously, unaware of the discomfort he was causing. It was the first time he had directed any conversation directly at her and Jenny immediately felt flustered. 'Sweets for the sweet,' he said softly, teasing her and trying to make her smile. Jenny coloured brightly; he seemed to be immune to the atmosphere he was creating or the depth of pain he had caused her.

'I don't normally——' she began, just managing to keep her voice under control.

Pablo cut in immediately, his eyes dancing as he flirted outrageously, 'You look lovely, even more lovely than I remember you. Join me in a...' He paused while he scanned the menu. 'A crème brûlée.' He smiled triumphantly at the waiter, giving Jenny no time to object. Thaddeus looked at Jenny, awaiting her protest, but there was none and his eyes narrowed with unconcealed contempt. Jenny's pulse quickened and her heart beat faster as Thaddeus said spitefully, 'Someone told me you were too weight-conscious to eat desserts.'

Jenny's eyes darted to his, pleading for his silence. She was unable to read his thoughts in those depths. She felt a rush of colour to her face as she recalled how much he knew about her and Pablo.

The meal was tearing Jenny into shreds. She felt she was caught between the devil and the deep blue sea. Her eyes constantly strayed to the grim look on Thaddeus's face and she struggled hard to speak normally to Pablo. Though he was kind and attentive, it only increased Jenny's turmoil. She was grateful that Pablo seemed unaware of how badly she had taken their break-up. It was like meeting an old friend, and he seemed determined only to recall happy times.

They had many happy memories to share and Jenny felt herself relaxing in his company despite herself. Margaret kept an easy flow of conversation going, carefully redirecting anything that might open old wounds, and Jenny smiled gratefully at her sister for her tact and diplomacy. Jenny tried to forget all about Thaddeus but she could not help but notice the ominous fury that was building in his eyes. He obviously wanted to talk business, and Jenny was preventing this by talking to Pablo about old times. Thaddeus's main concern was the film, and he disliked wasting time on futile conversation.

She decided it was best not to wait for coffee. She wanted to escape to her room as soon as she could; she felt exhausted. The strain of the meal had been far too much; the whole evening had been a frightful ordeal. She had hated being in such proximity with Thaddeus, feigning indifference to him when her whole being ached for him. She knew that was pointless, it was all a well practised sham on his side—yet another poor female had fallen victim to his charm.

She was totally aware of the change in Thaddeus, could sense his hostility and bitter anger even if he took pains to conceal it from the others. Jenny didn't feel safe and wanted to put as much distance as she could between them. She was frightened by the brooding darkness in his eyes and the firm stiffness of his jaw.

'If you all don't mind, it's been a hectic day for me, and I really must get to bed,' she said, pushing back her chair. She gave a weak smile all round, carefully avoiding Thaddeus's face. The others nodded their approval and wished her goodnight.

'I'll see you to your room, Jennifer.' Thaddeus's voice was chillingly formal and Jenny knew better than to object. Instead she smiled sweetly, and waited for him to join her. When they got there she opened her room door and turned to thank Thaddeus, but he pushed her roughly inside and snapped on the lights.

'You really enjoyed that, didn't you?' he drawled, leaning against the door till it closed behind him. Jenny turned away, her body stiffening with intense dislike and anger. There was a brief pause, during which the tension increased rapidly till Thaddeus snapped again.

'Well, why didn't you tell me your sister was Margaret Miller?'

Jenny gave him a sharp, irritated glance over her shoulder. 'It's because it was none of your business.'

He gave a derisive smile. 'It is my business,' he retorted, his eyes flaring with a flicker of temper. 'This job unfortunately seems to depend upon *your* relationships,' he sneered, his stance dangerously threatening.

'That's your own fault. I told you all along I didn't want this job, but you insisted. Tricking me with your lies, even going to...' She stopped as she saw his expression change and her body iced over. She took a step back, already trembling as he approached with a lean stride, taking her into his arms and crushing his lips against hers. His mouth took hers, at first angry and forceful, pushing her lips apart as the kiss deepened. Then suddenly it changed, as if all the anger had gone. His lips became gentle and persuasive, coaxing a response from her already weakening body.

Her pulses leapt in confusion as she allowed his long fingers to slide over her shoulders, pushing her gently back on to the chair. Jenny's legs buckled but he supported her weight as he lowered her down carefully, his lips never leaving her mouth. She began to kiss him back, her mind swimming, making her feel dizzy and out of control. Thaddeus raised his head, his eyes glittering.

'Who is it you want, Jennifer—me or Pablo? Or maybe both of us,' he murmured drily, and Jenny's eyes flicked open in disbelief at his words, her body chilled to the bone as the full meaning of his words sank in. She stared at him, her face white and angry.

'How dare you?' she breathed through tight lips. He laughed at her outrage with amusement.

'Ah, but I do dare,' he drawled. 'I saw you tonight, hanging on to his every word like a lovesick schoolgirl.'

Jenny was furious. 'Get out!' she spat at him, hating the very sight of him. Thaddeus raised one dark, winged brow.

'I suppose I'd better leave before Pablo arrives,' he said with a derisive smile as he ran one long finger down from her cheek to her mouth, parting her lips sensually.

'I've told you to get out,' she said tightly.

Thaddeus laughed under his breath, his mouth parting to reveal his white teeth. 'So you did,' he drawled, not moving an inch.

Jenny stared at him with incredulity, seeing the hungry expression in his eyes. Her breath caught in her throat. Then Thaddeus gave a shrug of his powerful shoulders and turned and left. Jenny darted immediately for the door, snapping the bolt across and turning the key to ensure no one else could enter tonight.

The shrill ringing of the telephone pierced the deep sleep that Jenny had finally fallen into and she gazed in horror at her travel alarm. She groaned as she snatched up the phone. 'Hello?'

'We were supposed to settle arrangements with the government officials today,' Thaddeus's grim voice barked down the line, awakening Jenny immediately.

'Yes, yes, I know—I'll be down in a minute,' she reassured him quickly as she clambered from her bed. The sheets, still warm, seemed to beg her to stay, but she ignored them. She splashed some cool water over her face to waken herself up and dressed with amazing speed. She had no time to shower and grabbed a piece of fruit from her bowl for her breakfast as she rushed down the stairs.

Thaddeus was pacing impatiently in the foyer and he looked up as he heard her footfall on the stairs.

'At last!' he muttered, making for the door, and Jenny had to run to catch up with him. She avoided his eyes, unable to face him after last night. Now she had seen Margaret and everything was settled, maybe he would allow her to return to England.

'Has Margaret agreed to do the film?' she asked as they got into a taxi, casting a glance at his face. He nodded but said nothing, just stared out of the taxi window and into the passing streets. It was useless to ask him now, she thought; he would be in no mood to listen. He seemed preoccupied with other thoughts—probably the forthcoming production. How she hated his self-centredness.

The next few days seemed to pass in a whirl. Filming was due to commence and Jenny was rushed off her feet trying to organise everything from refreshments on site to making sure the police kept the sightseers far enough away from filming that they did not appear in shots. It was a hectic pace, and Thaddeus had returned to his role as director with relish. No one seemed safe from a sharp lashing from his tongue.

As usual it was Jenny who fared worse than anyone. It was only because her sister was there that she endured

it without complaint. She was also grateful for the kind
words of Pablo.

They were filming in the port area, there were hundreds
of extras and the place was teeming with crew members.
Jenny had been up since five o'clock, carefully seeing
to everything, and now, five hours later, she was beginning to tire.

She sank exhausted on to a large bail of rope and
fanned herself with her sheaf of papers. Although it was
only ten o'clock, it was already hot, and the heat certainly did nothing to improve Thaddeus's temper. His
roaring voice seem to carry in the air.

'Hello, Jenny, how's tricks?' a friendly voice asked,
coming up to her. Jenny looked up and drew back at
first, before smiling.

'I didn't recognise you at first. You make an excellent
pirate king,' she enthused as she looked intently at the
clever make-up and colourful costume Pablo was
wearing. She had grown accustomed to seeing him, and
it was with slow realisation that she had come to terms
with her feelings for him.

Looking back, she realised he wasn't to blame. He'd
just compounded a problem that had been already there.
She had felt unloved and unwanted, struggling through
adolescence on her own. If anything, the break-up of
their relationship had made her cry for help—though in
a desperate way, she acknowledged, grateful it was all
behind her.

'And do you feel safe with such a desperate man?'
Pablo teased, moving closer and stroking his false beard
like an actor from a Victorian melodrama.

She laughed. 'Quite safe,' she acknowledged with a
smile, knowing that she was fully over him. She knew

she was—all her emotions were now fully spent on Thaddeus. Pablo looked at her in mock horror.

'Ssh—you'll ruin my reputation,' he admonished her, placing his fingers on his lips. They both laughed, unaware that Thaddeus was storming towards them, his eyes narrowing as he saw them together. He pushed his hands deeper into his trouser pockets as he marched over.

'You're wanted in this next scene,' he barked at Pablo, but directed his gaze at Jenny.

Pablo wasted no time; he was very professional and he quickly ran across the dock, leaving Jenny to face Thaddeus alone. The sun blistered down on Thaddeus's face, the sunlight glinting on his raven-black hair, his eyes as cold and clear as the sky above.

'Haven't you any work to do?' he drawled.

Jenny stayed where she was, held immobile by the dark fury in his eyes. 'Is there anything you want me to do? If not, I'm free at the moment.'

He smiled slowly. 'There's lots you could do for me, but I suppose I'd better wait till you have finished with Pablo,' he taunted.

She tried to push past him but his powerful body blocked the path.

'Excuse me,' she said tightly, not even looking at him.

His hand coiled around her wrist. 'I want to talk to you,' he said grimly. Jenny couldn't understand his tone; it was strangely at odds with the expression on his face.

'Then get in the queue,' she spat, pulling herself free and marching away. She hated him, she strode away muttering to herself, till Thaddeus's voice barked,

'That's a wrap.'

Filming stopped immediately at his command and everyone began to disentangle themselves from cos-

tumes and make-up. Jenny was busy once again ensuring everyone had the right schedules, plus all the
minor irritations of the job: small bills to pay, a doctor
needed calling due to a case of sunstroke. It was another
full three hours before she had finished work, and she
was shattered.

She opened her bedroom door. It was dark, for the
shutters were still closed, making the room feel lovely
and cool. Her bed was already turned down, inviting
Jenny's tired body to fall asleep immediately. She lay on
top of the bed in the cool darkness, enjoying the peace
and silence, and closed her eyes. But then she snapped
them open at once.

'Who's that?' she called as she heard her door open.
'It's only me, Sis,' was the reply—and for a moment
Jenny was disappointed.

'Come in,' Jenny answered, getting up and throwing
open the shutters, flooding the room with light. 'It's hot,
you know; the temperature is far higher than is usual at
this time of year.'

'Is it?' Margaret asked, unconcerned by the heat.

'Yes—we had decided to film now so that it would be
easier,' she explained, sitting back down on the bed.

'We?' Margaret queried, a smile toying at her lips.

Jenny cast her an irritated glance but remained silent,
ignoring her sister's bait.

'You love him, don't you?' Margaret persisted, a trace
of hope in her voice. Jenny's head darted up and she
flashed a look of anger at her sister.

'I certainly do not. If anything, I hate him.'

'"The lady doth protest too much, methinks,"'
laughed Margaret, and Jenny threw a pillow at her.

'Is it that obvious?' Jenny asked, suddenly realising she was probably the butt of everyone's jokes. She looked anxiously at her sister.

'No,' she said, shaking her head. 'Only to me,' she added wisely. Jenny sighed audibly.

'It's rather one-sided, I'm afraid, but don't worry—I'm not about to take any drastic steps. That's all in the past now,' she reassured her sister, seeing the anxious look on her face.

Margaret nodded. 'And Pablo?' she asked. 'Is he in the past?'

'Yes—yes, he is. He's a friend, nothing more,' Jenny informed her, and it was at that moment that she realised it really was true.

'I'm glad. We've been working together a lot in the States—mini-series, things like that,' Margaret told her sister, but Jenny picked something up in the older woman's tone, and she looked at her with a puzzled expression.

'And?' she asked, smiling.

'We're—planning to get married.' Margaret rushed the words out, and Jenny sat stunned for a moment before wrapping her arms around her sister and hugging her with delight.

'Congratulations! I'm delighted for the both of you. We should celebrate.'

'You're pleased?' Margaret asked, still a little unsure.

'Of course! Let's have dinner tonight to celebrate,' Jenny enthused, determined to show her sister how pleased she was.

'Yes, that will be lovely—but let's keep it a secret. It will become a circus if people find out,' she told Jenny as she stood to leave.

'You're right—I was forgetting how famous you both are,' Jenny laughed as she fell back on the bed.

Jenny lay in the silence of her room, her mind in a turmoil. It seemed so strange to think of Margaret married, especially to Pablo, but they were made for each other. They both were brilliant in their field and understood the demands of their careers. Jenny knew she couldn't possibly cope with the constant high life.

She sighed, her mind drifting back to her little cottage. She had just admitted to her sister that she loved Thaddeus, but he had made more than plain his feelings for her. Tears threatened to fall, but Jenny blinked them away. She would just have to cope and make sure she kept her feelings well hidden.

She fell into a dream-filled sleep studded with vivid images of Thaddeus and her back at the cottage in the summer months, sharing picnics and laughing. It was late evening before she woke up. She remembered her dinner date instantly and wanted to look her best. She had brought nothing really dressy except her silk dress, and she couldn't wear that again. She rummaged through her wardrobe in desperation. Then an idea struck her. She had spotted a beautiful dress in the hotel shop. The price-tag was exorbitant, but Jenny suddenly didn't care—she needed cheering up, she decided, and snatched up her bag, determined to buy it.

She waited patiently as the shopkeeper folded the dress with care, wrapping it up carefully in tissue paper.

'Going somewhere special?' a voice drawled behind Jenny, and she stiffened immediately, the hair on the back of her neck rising and her stomach somersaulting at the unmistakable sound of Thaddeus's voice.

'Y-yes,' she stammered back, not turning round and willing the shop assistant to hurry.

'Rather different from the usual things you wear,' he commented drily as he paid for his paper, his eyes flicking over her.

Jenny felt herself colour under his cold scrutiny. She remained silent; it was none of his business what she wore, she thought angrily, taking the bag from the assistant and hurrying to the door. He was at her side in moments.

'I want to talk to you,' he reminded her forcefully, and Jenny stopped in her tracks, turning to face him. She was angry and saw no reason to hide it. But although her tone was sharp she managed to keep her face calm, unwilling to let him see her lose control.

'I can't think of anything we need to discuss,' she pointed out.

Thaddeus studied her for a minute, his body still, the lithe, well muscled contours of it clearly defined in his snug jeans and white shirt.

'A director and his personal assistant always have matters that need discussing,' he said. Jenny's heart sank as she realised that once again she had put a personal interpretation on his desire to talk to her. 'Well?' he snapped, obviously irritated by her.

'When?' Jenny snapped back, frowning as she saw his jaw tighten at her attitude, but caring little.

'Now!' he barked, standing directly in front of her, his physical strength making her feel vulnerable as he looked down on her, his face holding an aggressive frown.

'It's not really convenient...' she began, but the warning look that flashed in his eyes silenced her objections at once. 'I'll fetch my pad,' she said in a resigned tone, climbing the stairs with a weary heart.

'I'll come to your room,' he informed her, and Jenny didn't bother to object. She wasn't interested any more.

'Pablo!' she cried as she opened her door, stunned for a moment when she saw a man in her room.

'Jenny! Margaret has told you the news?'

'Yes. Congratulations. I'm so happy for the both of you,' she said, swinging her arms around his chest. He hugged her back.

'Thanks,' he said, planting an affectionate kiss on her cheek.

The door opened and Jenny froze. She knew without turning who it was and the interpretation he would put on it. Pablo released her gently and said unwittingly, 'Dinner at nine,' as he left, smiling broadly as he closed the door.

Thaddeus said nothing. His face looked dangerously menacing and his eyes were flaring with a brightness she had not seen before. He watched her, his body still, as he tried to control his unleashed anger. Jenny backed away from him, sensing his anger but not understanding it.

'You don't understand...' she began, swallowing the rising lump of panic in her throat.

'Explain, then,' he challenged softly through clenched teeth as he approached her. Jenny moved further back till the bed prevented her from going any further and she rested her legs against it for support.

'I can't.' She suddenly remembered, the engagement had to be kept a secret. Her throat was tight and dry.

'Really? That does surprise me,' he drawled mockingly. He was closer now—too close—and Jenny felt herself begin to tremble. She was angry with herself for reacting like this. It was none of his business, and she immediately gained strength as she thought that.

'It's personal, and my private life is my own,' she told him, trying to keep the tremor from her voice and failing.

'Wrong!' he snapped. 'I've a multi-million-pound production going on here and I won't have it ruined by you.' His eyes ran over her with contempt, his mouth an angry line.

Jenny was furious. He wasn't jealous of her and Pablo; all he cared about was his blasted production.

'What makes you think I'd ruin it?' she retorted, her eyes glittering in the tense, angry silence. 'He'll probably do the love scene even better,' she remarked, hoping that would bother him, and for a moment she thought she had hurt him, but the expression on his face had been so fleeting that it was hard to tell. Thaddeus's eyebrows rose and a wicked smile played on his lips.

'I saw the tuition you were giving and it looked a little tame to me,' he sneered dangerously, and Jenny regretted her flippant remark. She stared at him in silence and felt the rapid beat of her heart quicken, her pulses thudding in an ever-increasing rhythm. Thaddeus slipped his hand deftly around her wrist and raised his eyes to hers as he felt her quickening pulse with a smile of amusement.

'You seem nervous,' he mocked.

Jenny's heart skipped a beat. 'N-no,' she stammered nervously, her voice holding no conviction. He watched her intensely, then his hands drew her slowly towards him, his fingers sliding around her waist as he bent his head, his mouth descending to hers. His lips brushed hers and her lids closed slowly as he teased her mouth for a few burning, agonising moments. Then they were clinging to each other, their mouths draining one other while Thaddeus's arms crushed her against him, moulding her body to his.

Jenny's head spun and she reached out, her hands sliding on his chest, feeling the rapid thud of his heart, the burning heat of his taut flesh. His mouth seared hers, his hands pressing into the small of her back as their kisses became more urgent.

Jenny could feel herself melting under his onslaught, her traitorous body weakening as his tongue began to tease her lips. She felt her legs buckle as he pressed her further back till she was lying on the bed. Her breasts heaved against his hard chest, her breathing rapid and ragged. Her hands tangled in his dark locks, drawing him ever closer to her, her body moulding seductively into his body as if they were made for each other.

His hands took hold of her head, his mouth clamped on hers with a burning passion, and a raging fire was burning within them both. He stroked over her breasts and Jenny groaned at his masterful touch. His hand slid sensually over her body, drawing her towards him, making her heart race out of control. He undid her blouse, popping the tiny buttons with a skilful hand, and she trembled as her blouse fell open and her lacy bra was revealed.

Thaddeus moaned softly, deep in his throat, and she shivered in anticipation as he lowered his head to her swelling breasts. His hot mouth teased against the edge of the lace, following the trail already scorched by his expert touch.

Jenny moaned softly, her body turning to liquid fire. He pulled her hands roughly upwards to release the clasp on her bra and he tossed it away, leaving her totally exposed. She trembled as he lowered her back on to the bed, his eyes gliding over her with unconcealed hunger. He stroked her erect nipples till she moaned with pleasure, and her body began to writhe as she sought satisfaction. Her breath caught in dizzy confusion as his tongue traced the tip of her nipple, and she arched her body against his. He held her close, his body hard against her yielding softness. He moved back to her lips, setting her body alight with flames of passion while his fingers caressed her breasts with increasing force.

He slipped his leg with ease between her thighs and the movement alerted Jenny. She was returning from the spiral of pleasure that had encompassed her body. She felt his strong hand descend to the rim of her shorts and stiffened immediately, pulling her head away from his hot lips.

She struggled away from him, twisting her body as she pushed him away, desperation making her strong. She snatched up her blouse, struggling to put it on. Her legs were shaking, her whole body shivering, and she felt her knees weaken at his furious look.

'It's a bit late for modesty,' he noted drily as she fastened the buttons on her blouse with trembling fingers. Jenny coloured at the humiliating remark but kept her head lowered. She was disgusted with herself for being so weak.

He stood up and came across to her, moving her awkward fingers and slowly fastening the buttons himself.

'I still want you, Jennifer,' he confessed slowly, his hands resting gently on her waist.

Jenny swallowed, her cheeks hot and flushed. 'But I don't want you,' she forced herself to say. Not like this, without love, without caring, she added silently. He pressed her chin, tilting her head back so he could see her face. His eyes darkened at her defiant, angry face, and a frown furrowed his brow.

'I think you're lying.' He paused for a moment while he considered his statement. 'No, I know you're lying. I felt your desire for me,' he said thickly, not moving his hands from her waist and pulling her slightly towards him.

Jenny shook her head as she tried to dismiss the truth of his words from her mind, and she pulled away from his hands, not trusting herself with him. Tears of hopelessness pricked the back of her eyes as she tried to suffocate her love for him.

'It's him, isn't it?' he demanded sharply, flicking his mass of dark hair from his face.

'Who?' she asked stupidly; the only man on her mind was Thaddeus.

'Pablo,' he snapped back grimly. Jenny shrugged her shoulders in a gesture of defeat. Let him think what he wants, she thought miserably, suddenly ashamed by her own behaviour, reacting like that to a man who cared nothing for her.

'You're a fool,' he spat at her venomously, his eyes narrowing to hard blue chips. 'He doesn't love you,' he said hoarsely. 'He'll just use you.'

Jenny's eyes shot open, staring at him as the heat left her body, leaving her filled with an unbelievable anger at his words. It seemed like the pot calling the kettle, to her.

'*He* will use me,' she ground out at him between clenched teeth, hate and dislike shining from her hurt, angry face. 'What about you?' she accused. Thaddeus was silent for a moment, watching her intently. His face drained of colour at her words, then he pushed her away and stormed from the room, slamming the door with such force that the whole room trembled.

Jenny sank on to the bed, feeling tired and defeated. The thought of going to dinner was the last thing she wanted, but she was determined to show Margaret and Pablo her pleasure at their news.

She pulled the new dress from its bag and viewed it critically. Thaddeus was right: it wasn't her usual type of dress—it was far too elaborate. It was a deep sapphire-blue, with a plunging back and a nearly as revealing front. A row of tiny sequins decorated the shoulders and the sleeves were full-length, fastening to a tight cuff. It was very elegant and sophisticated, and Jenny frowned as she placed it next to her body, turning critically as she viewed herself in the mirror. She pulled her hair up above her head and smiled. She might as well look as stunning as possible, she thought as she decided to wear her hair up.

She dressed with care, teased her hair up into a soft chignon and applied her make-up with a little more sophistication than usual. She smiled at the result. What a transformation! She looked totally different, and she felt it. She was going to enjoy herself tonight, to put all thoughts of Thaddeus Clarke firmly out of her mind.

She slipped her feet into the smart, heeled shoes that gave her an extra inch of height, and went down to the bar. There was already a number of people there, many of them members of the crew, and there was a ripple of comment as Jenny entered. She saw Pablo sitting in the far corner and made her way towards him. It was not until she drew closer that she could see he was with Thaddeus. She swallowed nervously as she approached, putting a flashily bright smile on her face. The two men stood as she drew level with the table and Jenny could feel the hot trail that Thaddeus's eyes were making over her body.

'Doesn't she look beautiful?' Pablo said softly with obvious appreciation. Jenny smiled her thanks, casting an oblique glance at Thaddeus. His face was cold and hostile as he looked at her, and she felt her throat tighten.

'Beautiful,' he drawled, and Jenny seemed to be the only one aware of the bitter acid in his tone. She flushed and sat down, aware of the cold inspection Thaddeus was making of her. 'I'll leave you two alone,' he said flatly, flicked a quick glance at Pablo, then his eyes rested on Jenny again.

She raised her eyes to meet his and shivered, her throat tightening when she saw the bitter anger there.

'Good evening,' he said with a veneer of politeness, inclining his head, and Jenny watched him stride away, longing to run after him and tell him the truth. But she remained silent. To do so, she knew, would make no difference to their relationship.

CHAPTER NINE

THE next few weeks had a very heavy schedule. Jenny was with Thaddeus every day and the atmosphere between them was strained to virtual breaking-point. Jenny felt herself growing more tired with every passing day. She felt really drained, a tiredness she had never experienced before, and the strain was beginning to show.

'I can't be in two places at once,' she snapped at one point as she rubbed her hand across her forehead to remove the beads of perspiration that were gathering there.

'I'm not asking you to be, just to get both jobs done as quickly as possible,' Thaddeus said, a grim finality in his voice as he glared at her. Jenny fought to keep her emotions under control, to appear calm despite the provocation.

'I'll try, but the change-over of crew starts today and that's going to take some sorting out,' she replied briskly, swallowing the queasy feeling in her stomach. She felt her head begin to swim, but she had never fainted in her life and wasn't about to start now. Thaddeus's eyes narrowed as he saw the colour drain from her face and her eyes sparkle a little too brightly. Jenny averted her eyes, unable to face the cold accusation in his eyes.

'Have you eaten this morning?' he demanded, his voice smoky and deep. Jenny moved—she was already feeling sick, without a confrontation with Thaddeus. That would only make matters worse.

He caught her by the arm so she could not leave, and Jenny felt too weak to struggle. He noticed her flaccid arm and a grim look of determination fixed on his face.

'Have you had breakfast?' he asked again, a little more softly. Jenny thought for a moment, then shook her head. She had been in such a rush that she hadn't even thought about breakfast. Anyway, the last couple of mornings she had felt too sickly to eat. The air was so oppressive and she awoke still tired. A niggling doubt was already beginning to form in her mind but the horror of it made her deny it. She kept trying to persuade herself that her sickness was due to the heat. Surely she couldn't be pregnant? She wondered if Thaddeus suspected, and what his reaction would be—not that she would ever tell him. She would never want to trap him into a commitment.

'Not as yet; I'll get something later when I've done this,' she reminded him, brandishing the papers he had just handed her at him. She still didn't want to eat; she felt sick, even worse than before.

Thaddeus's grip tightened and his voice became low and threatening. 'Forget those!' he snarled, snatching the papers from her. 'I'll do it myself. Meanwhile, make sure you have something to eat.' His eyes ran quickly over her face, a troubled look clouding their clear blueness. He smiled at her unpleasantly. 'I can do without you being ill,' he pointed out with a flick of his lashes which sent his gaze skimming over her trembling body.

'I'm not hungry,' replied Jenny quickly. 'It's this heat—it robs me of my appetite.' She wiped her brow again with a agitated gesture.

'Damn you, Jennifer! I couldn't care less whether you're hungry or not—you're going to eat,' he growled as he practically dragged her to one of the catering wagons and pushed her roughly on to a wooden seat, forcing himself next to her so that escape was impossible. Her hands clenched and unclenched at her side with frustrated temper. There was a tense, angry silence between them and his hard masculine frame was far too close to hers. He seemed threatening and dangerous and Jenny moved slightly further away. Thaddeus frowned at her action but said nothing.

'Egg and bacon twice with toast and coffee,' he snapped towards the counter, his eyes immediately flashing back to Jenny. 'You look tired,' he commented in a gentler tone, and Jenny's eyes darted up to meet his.

'I'm not surprised, the amount of work I have to do,' she retorted, her voice hard. She still couldn't forgive him for the way he treated her, and yet his very closeness had made her pulse-rate increase.

Thaddeus's face paled, a grim, hard look on his chiselled features, his mouth a thin line. 'Really?' he drawled mockingly as he shook his black head. ''Everyone else seems to be coping,' he observed drily. He caught her chin with his long, strong hand and thrust her head back, tilting her face towards him. The shrewd blue eyes focused on hers and a smile toyed at his sensual mouth. Jenny hated the way her treacherous body seemed to melt at his touch, and she stiffened, moving her head away with an impatient toss.

'Well, I'm not. It's this heat; it's making me ill,' she complained irritably, flicking a fly away from her face, her brow creasing with annoyance. She knew that was only a half-truth and she longed to have enough free time to go to the chemist. She needed to know for certain.

The thought of pregnancy was still only a hazy threat, she tried to reassure herself.

Thaddeus viewed her actions with a frown matching her own, and then he smiled tightly as breakfast was put before them. Jenny swallowed as she looked at the food. She was too hot, too nauseous to face it. She picked up her coffee and sipped it with care, trying to avoid the steely gleam in Thaddeus's eyes.

'Back to black coffee again,' he noted coolly, though his tone made the air crackle with electricity.

Jenny remained silent; all she could hear was the frantic beating of her heart. She picked up her knife and fork with heavy hands, a cold dread coming over her as the smell of the food hit her. She pulled back, looking at the plate with distaste. She had never really enjoyed cooked breakfasts; now she positively hated them. She swallowed again the bile that was rising in her throat; she felt sick. The egg looked undercooked and the bacon was full of fat.

She could feel Thaddeus's eyes upon her, burning her body as he stared at her. She refused to look up; she could imagine the cold fury that was building in his eyes. She wiped her forehead again, the warmth of the day increasing the feeble way she was feeling.

'For God's sake, eat, Jennifer. It's food, not poison,' he growled, pushing her plate closer to her, his eyes glittering with icy contempt.

'I really don't feel like it,' she confessed weakly, nibbling at a piece of dry toast.

Thaddeus's fist hit the table with such force that every item jumped with disapproval. Jenny's coffee splashed everywhere, staining the table with a sea of brown waves. She leapt up in surprise, her heart thudding painfully against her chest, her pulses racing when she saw the cold, ruthless look in Thaddeus's face.

'You're going to eat that if I have to feed it to you myself,' he roared, pointing his long finger at Jenny's plate, his sharp white teeth flashing against the deep tan he had developed. For a moment Jenny faltered and he immediately snatched up her knife and fork.

'Please, I can manage myself,' she pleaded, hating the thought of him feeding her and the audience it would attract.

'You'll eat?' he asked, his voice softer and strangely at odds with the furious look on his face. Jenny nodded silently as he passed her back her cutlery. She cut into the egg and watched with growing horror as the yellow yolk split across the plate. She shut her eyes and pushed the food in her mouth, swallowing immediately and gulping on her coffee to take away the taste. Thaddeus sat stony-faced, but the tension he was feeling was evident by the insistent hollow drumming of his fingers on the table-top. His black brows rose as he studied her, his gaze flicking over her slender body, but his sooty lashes carefully concealed whatever he was thinking. Jenny ate the egg and bacon without enjoyment. She felt sickened with every mouthful but she dared not leave a morsel. Thaddeus would be furious and she felt too ill too argue. All she wanted was to be away from him, to become immune to the man. It was probably impossible, she had to admit. No woman was immune; even now she had caught the covetous glances of other women. Some were more discreet than others, but they were all overawed. It wasn't just his good looks, it was his strength of character, his ruthless sexuality that excited them.

Jenny frowned. Despite trying to be dismissive she knew she too had fallen under his spell. She finished the last mouthful of coffee with relief and looked at Thaddeus. She was secretly pleased that he was so interested in her welfare and she gave him a weak smile just before he dashed all her hopes.

'I hope you're eating properly. I've enough to do without nursemaiding a PA who should know better,' he informed her, a nerve still throbbing at his temple.

Jenny felt her heart sink. She looked at him with contempt and replied, 'I can assure you, Mr Clarke, I am more than capable of looking after myself.' Then she swallowed again as a wave of nausea passed over her. Her stomach seemed to have taken on a life of its own and was tossing about inside her at a terrifying pace. Thaddeus gave a slow smile of derision, his face swaying before her as she tried to focus on him. Jenny felt her pulse quicken, increasing the sickness she was feeling. He gave a low, almost cruel laugh.

'Capable!' he sneered as he shook his dark head, and his hand reached out and snatched her wrist in a tormentingly tight hold. 'You'd better be,' he warned in a low, menacing voice, 'because I'll be keeping a close eye on you, and I want to see you at every meal, every break, sitting and eating, and you can forget about using the workload as your excuse,' he snarled, anger etched on every inch of his face. Jenny felt herself trembling and she swallowed nervously, hating the swirling riot of emotion he seemed to be stirring up in her stomach. She felt a hot flush of heat throughout her body as she grew more and more nauseous. She stood to leave, gripping the edge of the table for support as she swayed. She had to hurry; she was going to be sick at any moment.

'You understand, don't you, Jennifer?' he said between clenched teeth, not relaxing his grip for a moment, his face darkening still further. Her eyes flicked to him and she opened her mouth to reply, but suddenly her stomach clenched in disapproval, and her throat was suddenly bone-dry. Jenny gave a moan as she pulled free of him and raced for the Portakabin, a handkerchief clutched to her mouth.

'Jenny!' he called, his voice hoarse and strangled, but she paid no heed. She felt desperately ill.

She leant against the cool wall of the little cabin ten minutes later. She had never vomited so violently in her life and she was troubled. It couldn't possibly be food poisoning, she reassured herself; they had brought their own catering team with them.

Jenny knew now, without the need for a test. The dull realisation that she could be pregnant was slowly becoming a grim reality. She went to the washbasin, turning her wrists over and over again under the running water. She splashed the icy water on to her face, trying to rid herself of the strange feeling that seemed to pervade her. She looked at her reflection in the mirror, gazing forlornly at the image before her. Though her eyes were bright, they were too bright, almost feverish, and her carefully acquired tan was barely visible, her features were so drawn and pale.

She brushed her hair from her face, tucking it behind her ears, and frowned. It made her look even worse. No wonder Thaddeus was annoyed; she was hardly a good advert for the company! Her frown deepened when she thought of him. She had hoped his attitude revealed a genuine concern for her; instead the truth of the matter was that he did not want the filming to be jeopardised in any way.

Jenny sighed audibly and picked up her bag, flinging it over her shoulder. It seemed heavier than usual and her shoulders sagged in protest. She had expected

Thaddeus to have returned to the job and she was startled to see him waiting for her.

'Are you all right?' he asked angrily, his mouth tightening. 'You have done this delib——' He broke off abruptly, his face grim, and he turned away. Jenny watched the back of his dark hair, the whorls curling gently; she could sense his anger.

'I'm sorry,' she said sadly, her eyes stinging with tears. It was all so unfair, she thought miserably; it wasn't her fault she felt sick, and she was still managing to complete everything he wanted done. He had no right to be angry. She looked back at Thaddeus as he turned. His face was rigid and a muscle jerked against his cheek as he sought to control himself.

'What are you so angry about? I've completed my jobs, not held up filming,' she informed him proudly. All feelings of nausea had left her now. She felt quite well—very well.

His face underwent a dramatic transformation—his eyes narrowed till they were like flints of ice and equally cold. For a moment his face was drained of colour, then his eyes seemed to reawaken, flashing with shards of icy temper, and his voice was biting and cruel. He looked at her with barely concealed contempt and spat at her hoarsely, 'Do you think that's all I care about?' his incisive blue eyes studying her.

Jenny faltered for a moment then nodded in agreement. 'Yes,' she said emphatically. 'I do.'

For a moment she thought he was going to strike her, he looked so angry, then he just shrugged his shoulders.

'That's right, and if this filming loses one hour because of you I'll make you pay,' he growled furiously before marching away, leaving Jenny hurt and bewildered.

She made her way back to the hotel, still thinking about Thaddeus. Despite everything she knew she cared for him. The hotel was alive with journalists, making it impossible to reach the desk without a struggle. She pushed her way through the heaving wedge of bodies.

'What's all the fuss?' she asked the distraught receptionist, who looked as if she was about to cry.

'It's those film stars—there's a rumour that they're to wed,' she explained as she darted away to answer the phone.

Jenny groaned. How awful—poor Margaret and Pablo; they would be persecuted no end. The journalists would follow them everywhere, and filming would become impossible.

Jenny's hand flew to her face; she had to speak to them. A suitable solution had to be found before filming was delayed. Jenny couldn't bear to imagine what Thaddeus would be like if his precious film was halted.

She rushed to her sister's room but it took several minutes to convince Margaret that it truly was her. Finally her sister opened the door and peered around.

'Thank goodness—come in,' she whispered as Jenny slipped inside. 'Have they gone yet?' she asked breathlessly.

'No, and I doubt they will without a story,' Jenny told her sagely. The room was larger than hers, a real star's room, and Jenny felt a momentary stab of hostility, until she remembered that at least she was free to come and go without the Press taking an interest.

'She's right,' agreed Pablo. 'So much for keeping it a secret,' he sighed, flopping back on the bed and resting his arms behind his head.

'Well, you can't stay here all day. There's a night shoot tonight with you two, isn't there? Thaddeus will be furious if anything interferes with that.'

'Yes,' mumbled Margaret without enthusiasm, 'the dramatic love scene, where he sweeps me in his arms and kisses me passionately.'

'I always kiss you passionately,' put in Pablo in a disgruntled voice.

'Ssh, you two—I'm thinking,' said Jenny thoughtfully, an idea formulating in her mind. 'I've got it. It's a risk but I think it's worth a try. But it has to be our secret; no one must know the real truth, not even Thaddeus.' Her eyes were troubled; it might cause more problems than it would solve, but it would definitely put Margaret and Pablo in the clear.

Jenny explained her idea to them carefully and it was greeted with much delight.

'It's great—when do we put it into practice?' asked Pablo, itching to start, a boyish, mischievous grin on his face. Jenny looked at him and smiled. It seemed hard to imagine that she had loved him once. She had changed so much, grown and matured, yet there was still a lot of little boy left in Pablo.

'There's no time like the present,' answered Margaret, pulling a comb through her hair. 'This will be our best performance,' she laughed as she opened the door.

'Break a leg!' called Pablo as he grinned at Jenny. 'Now, you'd better come here; I think the bed is the best place to set up this act.' He laughed as Jenny fell on the bed next to him, waiting.

Within moments the door flew open, and Margaret stood there with a flock of newsmen. She was about to give them an interview on her engagement. She paused for full effect, giving a gasp, then, her eyes blazing with outrage, she pulled at the ring on her finger and flung it dramatically across the room. The camera lights flashed hungrily in an attempt to capture every emotion.

'You stinking, rotten two-timer!' shouted Margaret indignantly, and Jenny drew back, amazed at her sister's ability. She certainly was convincing.

'My love,' crooned Pablo, pushing Jenny aside and catching Margaret's hand. 'She means nothing to me.'

'Get your hands off me! The engagement's off; I never want to see you again,' Margaret spat, pulling away and marching towards the lift as the journalists stood, not knowing whom to question first. Pablo made the decision for them by slamming the bedroom door so that they fled after Margaret, questions being fired from all sides.

'It worked,' roared Pablo, laughing as he fell on the bed and caught Jenny in his arms.

They both were too busy laughing to hear the door open, and the first time they realised Thaddeus's presence was when he barked, 'The Press were right for once.' His mouth curled into a derisive smile.

Jenny bit her lip and struggled to a sitting position. She was about to speak when Thaddeus continued. 'We'll see just how good your acting abilities are,' he sneered at Pablo. 'I'm still shooting that love scene tonight, and you and Miss Miller had better look convincing,' he snarled before slamming the door shut.

Pablo fell into a helpless heap of laughter, but somehow Jenny suddenly didn't feel like laughing any more.

'Look, I think we should have dinner together, just you and me. The Press are bound to be interested and it will certainly put them off the scent if we're seen together,' Pablo suddenly said seriously.

Jenny was unsure; she didn't want to take it too far, but it did seem logical. 'OK,' she agreed reluctantly as she went to the door. 'Best have dinner here at eight. We both still have to work tonight,' she reminded him grimly, suddenly recalling the thunderous look on Thaddeus's face. She only hoped Margaret and Pablo worked well tonight. If they didn't, she would surely be to blame.

Jenny was nervous. She could hear the Press still cluttering up the foyer and was not looking forward to being the centre of attraction. She swallowed nervously as Pablo slipped his arm through hers.

'To battle, fair maiden.' He grinned infectiously and Jenny laughed as she braced herself for the onslaught.

No sooner did they appear at the top of the stairs than a cry went up. A body of people swarmed towards them and Jenny stiffened with alarm. She smiled politely, dumbstruck as the barrage of questioning began. Lights seemed to be flashing everywhere, till she was nearly blinded, but despite the hundreds of flashing lights and the milling faces Jenny could still see only one—Thaddeus. He seemed to stand out, drawing her eyes towards him as if in a hypnotic trance.

She met the look of fury in his eyes and flinched at the brooding hatred she saw there. The descent down the stairs was impeded by the journalists pushing and shoving, and Jenny was grateful that she wasn't her sister. This certainly wasn't any fun, and she wondered how Margaret could stand it.

Pablo seemed delighted by the attention, swinging a possessive arm around Jenny's shoulders for extra impact and drawing her even closer. Thaddeus's eyes narrowed on them at his action and Jenny felt a *frisson* of fear as

she saw him approach. There was a thunderous look on
his face, as if he wanted to hit Pablo. Anyone putting
his film in jeopardy certainly annoyed him.

'I hear congratulations are in order,' he drawled
mockingly, his eyes gliding over Jenny. She had dressed
simply, knowing it was work tonight, and the cotton dress
of pale blue was ideal.

Thaddeus's eyes did a full inventory till he fixed his
gaze on her dilating eyes. She gulped, unable to speak,
her throat was so dry.

Pablo smiled warmly, kissing Jenny lightly on the
cheek as he accepted Thaddeus's congratulations. Jenny
coloured and darted a quick look at Pablo—she didn't
want this to be taken too far. Her eyes then quickly
flicked to Thaddeus, who looked grim and made his way
into the restaurant, the strain evident in his angry stride.

It was impossible to enjoy the food set before her. She
felt like a goldfish in a bowl—too many journalists had
immediately entered and surrounded them, watching
their every move with a bizarre interest. Though every
dish was cooked to the highest of quality, Jenny felt too
miserable to eat. She allowed Pablo to choose the meal,
taking little interest; she was too aware of the micro-
scope she was under. Yet of all the eyes it was the staring
eyes of Thaddeus who seemed intent on her every move.

The first course was a simple dish of seafood pre-
sented on a bed of fresh herbs and salad; for the main
course Jenny managed to eat a little of her chicken, but
the sauce seemed too strong for her taste. She frowned
as she scraped the elaborate sauce from the chicken
breast. She normally enjoyed spicy sauces, but not any
more. It's this cursed heat, she grumbled to herself.

Fresh forest fruits were simple enough for her to manage, though normally she avoided strawberries, for they often caused her to break out in a rash.

Suddenly Pablo picked her hand and kissed it passionately, whispering, 'Have to keep up appearances.'

Jenny nodded in agreement, smiling at his boyish grin and the obvious delight he was experiencing. A dark shadow suddenly fell across the table and Pablo drew back, a sullen look of resentment on his face as he looked up and saw Thaddeus.

'I shall need my PA in ten minutes,' he said frostily, avoiding Jenny's face completely. Pablo nodded with reluctance, waited till Thaddeus had turned away and then pulled a silly face. The strain was too much for Jenny and she burst out laughing. The whole thing was getting completely out of hand.

She saw Thaddeus freeze at her laughter and stifled it immediately.

Jenny was glad to leave Pablo, eager to be away from the entourage of Press and back to the sanity of her job—well, reasonable sanity she corrected herself as she made her way to the beach. The beach was well lit, and the sea looked beautiful under the shining silver moon. It was the most perfect of romantic settings. The heavy sweet scent of jasmine filled the air with its perfume, and the fire that had been lit for the scene cast a warm red glow on to the white sand.

'You're here at last,' barked Thaddeus as Jenny made her way towards him, ignoring the controlled anger in his voice. 'Where's Pablo?' he demanded angrily as he realised she had come alone.

Jenny shrugged her slim shoulders, goading him and enjoying it.

'I expect he'll be here on time,' she reminded him in her most official tone. 'He usually is.'

His eyes leapt with temper at her reply, then his face twisted into a humourless smile.

'I admire your trust.' He paused before adding, 'Or is it stupidity?'

Jenny iced over, furious at his words.

'I trust him,' she answered simply, and grew more incensed when Thaddeus laughed in derision.

'Then more fool you. How long do you think it will last this time?' he reminded her cruelly, and tears of rage instantly sprang to Jenny's eyes. She blinked them away, but he had already seen them, the brightness of the lights shining on her eyes.

'Jennifer!' he said hoarsely, but she turned and ran, falling awkwardly over an electric cable. She gave a groan as she thudded down on the hot sand.

'Are you all right?' Thaddeus's voice sounded strange and for a moment Jenny was too numb to speak. 'Are you OK?' he demanded again, helping her to her feet. Jenny nodded, feeling quite queasy. 'Sit down!' Thaddeus commanded, pushing her down into his chair and frowning at her pale face. Jenny rubbed her forehead as the now familiar feeling of nausea swept over her. She closed her eyes, suddenly feeling drained, unaware of the cold inspection Thaddeus was giving her.

'You'd better stay there, seated, while we shoot this, since Pablo seems to have got here at last. Now we shall see how much acting ability they both have,' he commented drily as the cameras started rolling.

Jenny watched with interest as silence descended on set and everyone for those magical moments travelled back in time. Margaret was running frantically down the beach, her red hair billowing behind her, her ample cleavage swelling under the period dress. Tearing behind her came Pablo, barefoot and making confident strides. He caught up to her with ease, pulling her into his arms. She gave a cry of despair as he lowered his head and kissed her until they fell on to the beach.

'Cut!' shouted Thaddeus. 'Cut!' he roared again, but the lovers were too involved with each other to heed his cry. He turned round swiftly, the triumph on his face surprising Jenny.

'There,' he said, pointing to Margaret and Pablo. 'What more proof do you need?' he scoffed.

Jenny was going to confide in him, to tell him the truth, but somehow now she didn't think he deserved it. He seemed to be taking pleasure in what he understood as her rejection. Her eyes blazed with passion, and she leapt to her feet with such speed that for a moment she felt dizzy.

'Mind your own business!' she snapped, her eyes hostile and hurt. 'You don't understand,' she yelled, ready to march away.

Thaddeus clenched and unclenched his fists at his side, his eyes black with rage. He suddenly looked quite different, ruthless and menacing.

'*I* don't understand?' he bit out through clenched teeth. 'It's you who doesn't understand.' His voice was chillingly quiet. He made a grab for her, but Jenny moved away, her eyes bright with fear and anger.

'Jennifer!' She remembered him call as the warm blackness enveloped her and she felt herself sinking away.

Jenny moaned, her head falling on his chest. She caught the familiar scent of his aftershave and jerked away. Where was she? What had happened?

'Hold still, you damn fool!' Thaddeus growled, pushing her head back on to his chest. The steady rhythm of his heart was strangely reassuring and Jenny sank back into her dreamless state. He placed her quietly on to the bed, informing Margaret in a crisp tone that the doctor would be here directly. Then he turned on his heel and left.

It was a thorough examination and the truth began to dawn on Jenny before her worst suspicions were confirmed. The doctor smiled brightly and Jenny shut her eyes to block out the good news. It was too awful to contemplate. How could she not have realised sooner? She swallowed nervously, unable to think of anything, the same stunning thought racing through her mind. I'm carrying Thaddeus's baby. Our child. She smiled—she could see him as a father. Strong but fair, not enough patience, though. She grinned as she imagined the frustration he would have coping with a difficult two-year-old. Then she frowned: there was no way he could avoid knowing now. How on earth would he react to the news?

Then the door opened and all those thoughts quickly evaporated. Thaddeus stood at the doorway, casting a black shadow into her room. He seemed to loom large and Jenny felt herself shrink back, pulling the covers to her chin as she slid down the bed. He walked in, slowly, with a panther-like tread, and Jenny swallowed the dry lump in her throat. Her heart was thudding painfully in her chest and her breathing was shallow and erratic. She suddenly felt very ill again.

He stopped at the edge of the bed, his eyes as black as the night, his face set into an angry grimace. She closed her eyes, hoping to feign sleep, but he was in no mood to humour her.

'One actress in the family is enough,' he ground out, and Jenny's eyes shot open to face the seething gleam of rage in his eyes. She felt a rush of colour to her cheeks and her body shivered under his cold scrutiny. She moistened her lips to answer him, but was not allowed the opportunity.

'I heard the news,' he said, his voice bereft of any real emotion, and Jenny's heart sank. He was obviously not pleased.

'I thought you would be pleased,' she said, unable to think of anything else to say. He frowned, then his expression changed to one of disbelief.

'Pleased?' he echoed scornfully. 'You're a bigger fool than I thought,' he scoffed cruelly.

Jenny recoiled at his words; she could not have felt more pain if he had physically struck her. 'Do you think this makes any difference?' he questioned her, his eyes boring into hers with venom. Jenny stared nonplussed as the realisation dawned on her. She meant nothing to him, nor did their child. How could she have been so foolish as to ever believe it could have been anything different?

'I thought it might,' she confessed simply, amazed at the composure in her voice. He gave a grunt of derision and shook his head almost wearily.

'You're such a child, Jennifer,' he said, a little wistfully, and she felt hot pinheads prick against the back of her eyes at his attitude. She wouldn't cry; she wouldn't give him the satisfaction of knowing how much he had hurt her.

'Then I'd better grow up quickly; I'll have a child myself to bring up soon,' she retorted, hoping to make him feel guilty. He sighed again and moved to the side of the bed. For a fleeting moment in the dim light of her room she thought she saw a flicker of emotion on his face. He shook his head, his eyes trailing over her.

'Something will have to be sorted out,' he said coolly, running his hand through his thick hair in a gesture of overwhelming frustration. Jenny nodded.

'That's my problem, I think,' she answered a little too quickly.

'Not just yours,' he reminded her grimly, snapping off the light. 'You'd better get some rest,' he added in a softer tone as he left the room.

Jenny lay in the darkness. The blackness seemed to creep over her whole being and weighed heavy on her body. She drew an instinctive hand across her flat stomach. Spreading her fingers, she tried to send some sense of love to her unborn child to make amends for the cold rejection of its father. She had never felt so afraid and desolate in all her life—as if someone had switched the sun off and there would never be any light or warmth again. She turned on to her side, and closed her eyes as she tried to blank out the vivid picture of Thaddeus's luminous eyes, glaring at her. She shivered at the memory, then sighed, and hot, salty tears began to pump uncontrollably from her eyes. She sobbed and sobbed till she fell into a fitful sleep.

CHAPTER TEN

JENNY had been ordered to stay in bed for a couple of days. The doctor felt she was working too hard and the rest would do her good. She would have objected but she felt no desire to see Thaddeus. His temper certainly hadn't been improved since she had taken ill. On the contrary, he seemed worse than usual; his booming voice could be heard throughout the hotel. Jenny grinned to think she was safe from him for once.

By the third day Jenny was bored. Following the doctor's advice, she had taken a cup of weak tea and ate two plain biscuits before getting out of bed. It seemed to work and she no longer felt as sick as she had.

Filming was moving at a pace now; all the major outdoor scenes were complete and Thaddeus was concentrating on minor shots. The rest of the film would be completed in the studios, the sets already underway.

Jenny stiffened as she heard a knock on the door, placed her book down with care and looked up expectantly as she called, 'Come in.'

She tried to smile as Pablo entered, but her shoulders sagged and her mouth fell a little. She'd still hoped it would be Thaddeus, yet she had not seen him for days. Pablo noticed the disappointment on her face and sank down on the bed beside her, taking up her hand and giving it a squeeze.

'How are you feeling?' he asked, smiling, trying to help her forget. Jenny shrugged carelessly. She had never felt better physically, but her heart was heavy and she felt truly miserable. She looked at Pablo with pain-filled eyes. The silence of the room seemed to thud against her own ears with an eerie rhythm. He drew her into his arms, rocking her gently. He didn't understand what was going on, but he recognised hurt when he saw it, and wanted to send it all away. Jenny fell gratefully against him, enjoying the comfort of his arms.

She heard the gentle knock on the door and Pablo had told them to enter before she had disentangled herself from his arms. She glanced up and saw Thaddeus. She was going to move but Pablo held her to him as if to protect her from any more pain, and she was grateful for his action.

'I am sorry for interrupting,' he drawled in an amused tone, and his eyes travelled over her. She paled at the tone in his voice but remained silent, lowering her eyes to avert his gaze. 'I've been in touch with the company and they're sending out a replacement PA this afternoon,' he informed her crisply. Pablo leapt to his feet with indignation.

'What do you mean?' There was angry accusation in his voice.

'I mean that Miss Collins's services will no longer be required by the company and she may as well return to England,' he explained flatly, his eyes narrowing on Pablo as if he disliked him intensely.

'This is wrong...' began Pablo, distraught and unable to fathom the reasoning behind Thaddeus's behaviour.

Jenny intervened quickly—both of them looked fit to burst and she didn't want to be the cause of angry exchanges. 'No, it's OK, Pablo. I think it's for the best,' she reassured him.

Pablo shrugged his shoulders and looked at them both, puzzled.

'I'll go, let you both talk,' he said, casting a look of distaste at Thaddeus, but Thaddeus was too occupied looking at Jenny to notice. Pablo closed the door and Jenny faced Thaddeus alone. She tilted her head back to look him straight in the eye. She refused to show weakness, refused to let him see the love she had for him.

'Will you leave, then, or stay on here holidaying?' he asked expressionlessly.

'I suppose I'll go,' Jenny replied, though she was silently praying that he would beg her to stay, to be with him. Thaddeus shrugged his broad shoulders, avoiding her eyes. He looked away through the open window.

'It *will* be for the best,' he said in a flat tone bereft of any emotion. 'Won't it?'

Jenny wanted to scream no, that she couldn't bear to be separated from him, but the words died in her throat. She looked at him bleakly. The little bit of hope she had clung so desperately to was evaporating like the morning dew. She lowered her head, bent with the weight of sorrow. She had to keep hidden the pain in her eyes.

'Yes, I suppose it will.' Her heart shattered and she forced herself to give a wan smile. Thaddeus remained completely still, his face grim, his dark eyes unreadable.

'When is the next available flight?' she asked, her voice calm even though she was screaming inside with pain. He looked at her, his eyes dancing with flames of rage.

'I don't know and I don't care,' he bit out, thrusting his hand through his thick hair.

'Well, thanks a lot,' she snapped back, angered by his cool indifference. 'I'll sort myself out,' she said efficiently.

'Well, that is your job,' he reminded her distantly, his eyes burning with hostility.

'Was my job,' she retorted, tears stinging the back of her eyes as she realised how quickly he had replaced her. He shrugged his shoulders, his face blank as his eyes searched her face.

'I've told you before: if you can't stand the heat stay out of the kitchen,' he bit out at her through clenched teeth.

'And, if I remember rightly, I told you it was the chef I couldn't stand,' she retorted, her face full of pain and anger. He stared at her for a moment, a long, angry, furious moment when time itself seemed to stand still, then he turned on his heel and strode out of the room, pulling the door closed with a finality that made Jenny want to cry. She rang the airport immediately—she wanted to spend no more time here. When her flight was confirmed for the following morning she felt totally empty, dead to all emotions. She flung a suitcase on to the bed and began to pack with meticulous care. The longer it took, the better in some ways—she wanted to hang on to every last moment. She felt cold, a chilling cold which was the result of her broken heart. It was unbelievable; the whole situation seemed unreal, and yet the real horror was that it was true, so painfully true, she reminded herself, closing her case and snapping the locks together.

She collected together all her bits: magazines, papers, half-used bottles of suntan lotion, and tossed them in the bin. She checked the wardrobe and drawers again, then remembered the bedside cabinet. She opened the tiny drawer and the heavy perfume instantly filled her nostrils. Hot pinheads pricked the back of her eyes and they grew soft with sorrow. Carefully she picked up the nosegay. The silken ribbon had faded and the tiny buds were turning yellowy brown. Jenny stroked her fingers across the top of the tiny bouquet and swallowed the pain-lump in her throat.

She turned to toss it in the bin, but paused and, without thinking too much about her motivation, slipped it into her hand luggage between her purse and her passport.

A knock on the door disturbed her and she hastily stuffed the nosegay out of sight.

'Come in,' she said shakily as she tried to control the tears that were threatening to fall. Her heart jumped as the door swung open and Thaddeus walked in. His bright blue eyes alighted on her case immediately, a look of surprise fleetingly crossing his face.

'When is your flight?' he asked, and his voice sounded hollow, empty.

'Tomorrow—the early flight,' she managed to tell him, her eyes fixed on his face, still hoping, still searching for a glimmer of love. Her heart beat out its own death-knell when she could find no love there. She looked at him intently. This was maybe the last time she would see him, and she was determined to have his image perfectly impressed on her mind. She wanted to see every line, every contour with vivid detail.

Thaddeus stared at her, unperturbed by her close scrutiny.

'I never realised it would be so soon,' he acknowledged, sinking his hands deeply into his trouser pockets. She thought for a moment that he was going to come across to her, but then he stopped.

'Jennifer——' he began, then broke off abruptly.

'Yes?' She tried not to sound too eager but her pulse leapt in anticipation and her eyes flicked to his.

'Nothing—never mind,' he said dismissively, turning to leave. But she couldn't leave like this, always wondering what he was going to say.

'No, wait. What did you want to say?' She didn't care if she sounded desperate; there was a chance, and she felt a spark of hope. But he flashed his ice-cold eyes at her, his harsh face dark and brooding.

'Have a safe journey home,' he said in a clipped tone, giving her a wan smile.

Jenny watched him leave and her heart lurched painfully. She suddenly felt very weak and she sank on to the bed. It was so obvious that he cared little for her.

She couldn't bear the thought of going downstairs and was determined to have dinner sent up. She would have to go to bed early anyway, as it was an early flight, but Margaret insisted she come to dinner downstairs and Jenny was stunned by her reception. A goodbye party had been organised, a huge banner wished her luck, and there were balloons and streamers everywhere. A simple buffet was being served and there was even chilled wine.

'Thanks; it's very thoughtful of you,' gasped Jenny, about to cry. Her emotions were certainly playing havoc with her. Margaret looked stunned and shook her head.

'It's nothing to do with me, Sis—it's Thad's idea,' she explained, passing her a fruit juice. 'Alcohol is out from now on, I'm afraid,' she smiled. 'Me, an aunt!' she laughed as she disappeared into the throng.

Jenny's eyes darted nervously around the room; she had to find him to thank him. She knew it was an excuse—she just wanted to see him again, to hear his voice. It was ridiculous, the man had treated her shamefully, yet still her heart cried out for him.

He was nowhere to be seen, and though plenty of people came to her with good wishes she still only wanted

Thaddeus. It was getting late and the room was stiflingly hot, full of smoke, and some elements were getting decidedly rowdy.

Jenny slipped out on to the terrace where a cool breeze drifted up from the port, bringing in its wake the heavy perfume of jasmine. Jenny knew that if she lived to be a hundred she would always be transported back to Tunisia if she ever smelt jasmine. She shivered as the air became cooler, and wondered how long she had been out there, lost in her thoughts.

Suddenly a heavy, warm jacket fell on to her shoulders. The body-warmed silk falling around her bare arms, she turned to face Thaddeus. He had been out and was dressed impeccably in a black dinner suit, the jacket of which now hung over her shoulders, dwarfing her slim frame.

'You'll catch your death out here,' he said, his smoky voice deliciously welcome to her ears.

She smiled and confessed quietly, 'I was looking for you.'

His dark, winged brows rose in surprise and there was an expectant look on his face. 'For me? Why me?' He smiled till his dimples showed.

'I—I wanted to thank you.' She swallowed nervously, her body already becoming alive at his proximity, and she longed to be in his arms. 'For the party,' she finished, lowering her gaze in case her desire was apparent. He stepped closer, as if her body was sending out a secret message to his, and tucked his strong fingers under her chin, pulling her face up so that he could see into the golden depths.

'It was the least I could do. You were the best PA I ever had,' he said, and his voice held a warmth that sent her head reeling. She looked at him and began to drown in the deep blueness of his eyes. She knew he was going to kiss her and she welcomed it. She clung to his shoulders, drawing him close till his handsome face was a blur. She stretched up, pulling his head towards hers while she stood on her tiptoes. Their lips met hungrily and he did not resist her passion.

She closed her eyes to capture the dreamy quality of his kiss. It was full of passion and she felt on fire, her body responding instinctively to his masterful touch, weakening with every passing moment. His hand caught in the silken tresses of her hair and held her head, preventing her from moving, and his mouth clamped on hers with a fierce possession. She could feel the savage hunger of his mouth against hers and her body turning into a molten fire of desire. His tongue pushed against her lips, forcing them apart until he could enjoy a closer intimacy with her.

Jenny forgot everything—her own conscious desire was for Thaddeus. She was lost in a hopeless vortex of emotion over which she had no control. They drew apart very slowly, almost reluctantly, and stood in silence, looking at each other with fiery intent. Thaddeus traced his long, seductive fingers gently across her now swollen lips, and Jenny shut her eyes tightly to hold back the tears that were threatening to fall.

She raised her hand and trapped his in hers, breathless and longing to hold on to him.

Then Thaddeus's features hardened, his eyes narrowed, and she felt herself ice over. She blinked back her tears as he exploded, 'Damn you, Jennifer Collins!'

She pulled back, hurt by his outburst and deeply shocked. She looked at him, all the hurt and pain mirrored clearly in her eyes. He looked back at her, his face still as cold, hard and unrelenting as ever, and her eyes filled with tears as he strode away, tossing a quick goodbye in his wake.

Jenny had been back at the cottage for over a month. She knew the job was coming to an end in Tunisia, as Margaret had kept in touch. She hadn't asked about Thaddeus—it would have been too painful—and Margaret was discreet enough to keep the conversation flowing without mentioning him.

It seemed like a million years since she had seen him, and the pain was still as fresh, like an open wound that refused to heal. She carried a physical pain in her chest, which ached continually. She had never imagined it would be this bad; she wanted him so much, to see him, hear his voice. Just to catch the familiar scent of him would be enough—but instead she had only memories, and not all of them were sweet.

She tried to think about her baby, about the new life growing within her, yet sooner or later her thoughts returned to Thaddeus. Every night before she fell into a dream-filled sleep he was her last thought, and she awoke early, sensing something was wrong. The sharp stab of reality would then pierce her as she realised she would never see him again.

She had never made her resignation final, but now she did. She couldn't face the possibility of seeing him and knowing they would never be together. It would be too painful to bear. She wrote her resignation as soon as she got back, explaining that it was due to ill health, and the company accepted it without query. Jenny knew she had to do something, though—she had a few savings but the cost of a new baby would certainly take most of them. She decided to take a job in the local restaurant, as a waitress; she knew she would only be able to work a few months but every bit of money helped.

She was quite surprised by how much she enjoyed her new job; it was close to home, she already knew everyone in the close community, and she certainly was not under the constant stress she had been used to. She was gaining weight; she tried to keep her diet as healthy as possible and a meal was always provided at the restaurant for staff—but it was the marvellous sweets that were her weakness. Since becoming pregnant her appetite had doubled, and she seemed unable to stop eating ice-cream with lashings of chocolate sauce.

Friday was always a busy night, but the sudden snowfall had forced many people to stay at home, and the threat that more was on the way was causing concern. No sooner had the last patron gone than the staff moved with speed, clearing away in record time. Jenny gratefully accepted the tub of chocolate-mint ice-cream and fudge sauce that the kind chef offered her. She knew he wanted their relationship to take a more personal turn, but Jenny just wasn't interested. No man could compare with Thaddeus.

She drove home determined to enjoy the dessert while watching TV. She drove slowly back to her cottage; the roads were icy and the snow was falling fast. She parked her car and went into her snug cottage. She had banked up the fire before she'd gone out, and there were still embers glowing. She tipped more coal on, flicked on the side-lamp and settled down in front of the TV.

She opened her huge tub of ice-cream with a smile and tucked her legs under her body. There was a gentle swelling in her stomach now, and she rested the carton on the tiny lump. She flicked from channel to channel— then stopped suddenly as the faces of Margaret and Pablo flashed on to the screen. Their news was out at last that they were to be married. They both seemed to thrive on all the media attention.

Jenny laughed as they revealed the little trick they had played on the Press. She was pleased it was all out in the open; she dreaded to think what a circus their wedding would be, but it was obviously what they both really wanted. Jenny finished the last of her ice-cream, giving the empty carton to Theo, who licked at it delicately with his pink tongue. He seemed to have become a permanent fixture since Jenny's return, and she was delighted with his company.

She fell into bed at last, tired but at peace. She was pleased to see her sister finally settled, and for the first time in a long while she slept well.

When she awoke, the silence of the day seemed to thud against her ears. She knew even before looking that there had been another tremendous snowfall. She was right: everywhere was covered in a dense, pure white blanket of snow, and Jenny was grateful that she didn't have to venture out.

She dressed in a baggy top and elastic-waisted ski-pants. The top flowed over her little bump, so it was hard to even tell she was pregnant.

Jenny passed the day lazily. She had begun knitting and was enjoying the results of her efforts: tiny bootees and little cardigans. She was enjoying her solitude again, and yet she knew that within months her single life would be gone forever and she would be a mother. She swallowed nervously at the thought. It seemed a tremendous responsibility to bring up a child alone; yet she had no other option.

She had begun to take a nap in the afternoons, and she curled up on her chair, closing her eyes while she listened to the gentle music washing over her. She had become used to Thaddeus's way of cooking, and prepared her evening meal in the morning when she wasn't as tired and let it cook very slowly in a low oven.

She awoke with a start. She had slept longer than usual and the room was in darkness. Someone was banging furiously on her door, and Jenny felt frightened.

She switched on the lamp, immediately gaining some comfort from the bright light. The banging was ceaseless—whoever it was was determined to gain entry. Jenny trembled; it was at times like this that she hated her solitude, and she felt oddly vulnerable now she was pregnant.

She crept cautiously to the door on tiptoe and peered out of the tiny window in the door, but she could see no one. Outside it was completely, ominously quiet. Jenny shivered and double-checked the locks.

As she went back into her tiny lounge, she gave a scream: a face was glaring at her through the window. She stepped back, her eyes filled with fear.

'For God's sake let me in, woman,' the familiar voice roared, and Jenny's stomach somersaulted as she recognised him. For a moment she was too shocked to move; she just couldn't believe it until his voice roared again, 'Open this door before I knock the bloody thing down.'

Jenny rushed for the door, her fingers fumbling with the locks, her hands were trembling so badly. At last she opened the door and there, looming in the doorway with a face of thunder, stood Thaddeus. She had hoped for a smile, for him to sweep her up in his arms and to tell her that they would never part. Instead he stood as if transfixed, staring at her, his eyes slowly dropping till they rested on the gentle swelling of her stomach.

Jennifer felt his gaze and instinctively folded her arms across her child for protection. He grimaced at her reaction and strode past her, flinging his coat over a chair in a familiar gesture. Jenny followed, her heart racing, her pulses leaping with a joy she tried hard to suffocate.

He stood in the centre of the room, his eyes cool and cynical as he viewed her.

'Sit down,' she managed to say, amazed at the composure in her voice when she longed to touch him, to feel his arms around her.

His eyes flicked over her, but his dark, sooty lashes hid the depth of his feeling.

'I'd rather stand,' he snapped back, his body visibly stiffening as he spoke.

'Suit yourself,' Jenny answered, trying to act unconcerned, and she sat back down herself, picking up her knitting. She had to do something with her trembling hands. There was a tangible silence for a moment while they both thought of something to say. It was Jenny who shattered the silence first. She had to know why he was here, what he wanted.

'Well?' She knew she sounded brusque, but she had to if she was going to survive. 'What do you want?' she demanded, keeping her eyes lowered, concentrating on her knitting. To look at his face would be a grave mistake—she knew that.

He didn't answer for a moment as he tried to formulate the words, then he snapped, 'Have you seen the news about your sister and Pablo?'

Jenny grinned. Surely he hadn't troubled himself to come all this way to tell her that? He noticed her amusement and frowned, his voice becoming sharper.

'You did know, didn't you?' His voice was angry now, and her eyes darted up to meet the hostility in his. Jenny was stunned by the anger on his face and she leapt to her feet in defence.

'Of course I knew,' she retorted, moving to the kitchen to make some coffee.

He followed her, snatching the kettle from her hand and glaring at her with such intensity that she felt afraid.

'When did you know they were to be married?' he demanded, banging the kettle down and facing her, his eyes as bright as cut diamonds.

Jenny sighed. What was he getting at? What difference did it make to him?

'In Tunisia—they told me then. Why?'

There was a gleam of triumph in his eyes which she couldn't fathom.

'Pablo told me that you were never lovers, that it was all a ruse for the sake of the Press.' His tone seemed to beg for reassurance and Jenny merely nodded. Yet he continued as if still doubting, 'But I saw both of you together.' He was half talking to himself, as if trying to solve a puzzle. Jenny's eyes darted to his, a flare of hope in her heart.

'We were never lovers and, yes, it was a ruse to put the Press off the scent, to give him and Margaret some privacy and to allow your precious film to be completed without hindrance.'

'Without hindrance? I've lost two days now. I've had to track down Margaret and Pablo. At first they were reluctant to see me, then I had to drive up here——' He would have continued, but Jenny interrupted.

'What do you mean, you had to see Pablo and Margaret?' she asked, puzzled by his behaviour.

'I wanted to see Pablo to ask him what on earth was he playing at, leaving you in this condition and marrying your sister!' exploded Thaddeus. He turned his back on

Jenny as he spoke and she was grateful, as it allowed her to smile.

'What did he say?' She began to splutter before she finished the sentence.

'Naturally,' barked Thaddeus, 'he was furious—they both were—and then they explained the awful truth.'

'Awful truth?' shouted Jenny, glaring at him. He spun round immediately, taking her fiercely into his arms.

'For God's sake stop misreading what I'm saying. I mean the awful mistake I had made.'

'You know the child is yours now,' she said carefully, 'but what on earth made you think it was Pablo's?' she asked, somewhat bemused.

'You did,' he snapped at her, still angry at her actions, which had caused all the misunderstanding.

'Me?' she echoed incredulously.

'Yes, that stupid idea of yours to fool the Press. Your morning sickness I interpreted as your desire to be super-slim again—for him. I was torn apart with jealousy and I hated myself and you for it. When the news was broken that you were pregnant I just couldn't believe it. I had to send you away. The pain that you were in love with someone else *and* bearing his child was more than I could bear,' he explained, his arms wrapping tighter around her as he drew her close, kissing her softly on the lips.

Jenny drew back, her world spinning; she felt dizzy. It was all so completely unreal. This actually meant he loved her.

'We've been such fools, haven't we?' she asked, seeking his approval, and he lowered his head to her, his hot breath caressing her face as he answered.

'Yes, we have—we could have lost each other,' he said sadly, holding her even tighter as if he never wanted her to go. 'There was never a day went by when I didn't think of you,' he admitted, with a smile that warmed her heart.

'And—fatherhood?' she queried, gaining confidence as she was held in his strong arms.

'Now that was a bit of a shock, I can tell you, but I'm delighted. More than delighted—thrilled,' he said, hugging her tightly then releasing her. 'We couldn't harm him, could we?' he asked, looking down on Jenny's gently swelling stomach.

'No, not at all,' she laughed, pulling him back into her arms but loving the genuine concern he was showing. She clasped him by the hand and drew him back into the lounge, where they both sat on the couch. His arm was wrapped around her waist, his hand gently stroking across her stomach, and he smiled at his unborn child. Jenny snuggled down closer to him and Thaddeus bent his head, his lips hot and possessive against hers.

It was like a new beginning, a fresh start. It was a kiss that was full of love for her and their child. It was deep and warm, full of unspoken desire, and Jenny wrapped her arms freely around his chest, drawing him close to her. Her body softened against him, yielding to his touch. Her heart was soaring beyond the stars as he trailed a burning row of kisses down her neck. The kiss was long and powerful, awakening in them both the desire for closer intimacy.

'Jennifer!' whispered Thaddeus huskily, his voice low and full of invitation. She looked up and saw the hungry look of love in his eyes. She smiled by way of reply.

'Later; I have to eat first,' she laughed. 'I'm constantly hungry.'

Thaddeus threw back his head and joined in the laughter. 'Have you thought of any names yet?' he asked, patting her stomach softly. Jenny nodded with enthusiasm.

'If it's a girl, Jasmine.'

He smiled, understanding the connection with Tunisia immediately. 'And a boy?'

'Nicholas.'

'Nicholas?' he queried, smiling at the mischievous grin on her face.

'After Old Nick—yet another name for the devil, and he certainly captured us!'

Thaddeus smiled, drawing her tightly into his arms and kissing her tenderly till she melted, her body moulding against his, fitting together with him like a perfect jigsaw. He drew back, kissing her lightly on the nose.

'I only hope it's a girl, then,' he smiled. She laughed softly, stroking his handsome face. Girl or boy—it didn't matter. They loved each other.

Next Month's Romances

Each month you can choose from a wide variety of romance with Mills & Boon. Below are the new titles to look out for next month, why not ask either Mills & Boon Reader Service or your Newsagent to reserve you a copy of the titles you want to buy – just tick the titles you would like and either post to Reader Service or take it to any Newsagent and ask them to order your books.

Please save me the following titles:	Please tick	✓
SIMPLY IRRESISTIBLE	Miranda Lee	
HUNTER'S MOON	Carole Mortimer	
AT ODDS WITH LOVE	Betty Neels	
A DANGEROUS MAGIC	Patricia Wilson	
TOWER OF SHADOWS	Sara Craven	
THE UNMARRIED BRIDE	Emma Goldrick	
SWEET BETRAYAL	Helen Brooks	
COUNTERFEIT LOVE	Stephanie Howard	
A TEMPORARY AFFAIR	Kate Proctor	
SHADES OF SIN	Sara Wood	
RUTHLESS STRANGER	Margaret Mayo	
BITTERSWEET LOVE	Cathy Williams	
CAPTIVE BRIDE	Rosemary Carter	
WILLING OR NOT	Liza Hadley	
MASTER OF NAMANGILLA	Mons Daveson	
LOVE YOUR ENEMY	Ellen James	
A FOOLISH HEART	Laura Martin	

If you would like to order these books in addition to your regular subscription from Mills & Boon Reader Service please send £1.80 per title to: Mills & Boon Reader Service, Freepost, P.O. Box 236, Croydon, Surrey, CR9 9EL, quote your Subscriber No:................................. (If applicable) and complete the name and address details below. Alternatively, these books are available from many local Newsagents including W.H.Smith, J.Menzies, Martins and other paperback stockists from 13 August 1993.

Name:..

Address:..

....Post Code:..........................

To Retailer: If you would like to stock M&B books please contact your regular book/magazine wholesaler for details.

You may be mailed with offers from other reputable companies as a result of this application. If you would rather not take advantage of these opportunities please tick box ☐

4 FREE
Romances and 2 FREE gifts just for you!

You can enjoy all the heartwarming emotion of true love for FREE! Discover the heartbreak and happiness, the emotion and the tenderness of the modern relationships in Mills & Boon Romances.

We'll send you 4 Romances as a special offer from Mills & Boon Reader Service, along with the opportunity to have 6 captivating new Romances delivered to your door each month.

Claim your FREE books and gifts overleaf...

An irresistible offer
from Mills & Boon

Become a regular reader of Romances with Mills & Boon Reader Service and we'll welcome you with 4 books, a CUDDLY TEDDY and a special MYSTERY GIFT all absolutely FREE.

And then look forward to receiving 6 brand new Romances each month, delivered to your door hot off the presses, postage and packing FREE! Plus our free Newsletter featuring author news, competitions, special offers and much more.

This invitation comes with no strings attached. You may cancel or suspend your subscription at any time, and still keep your free books and gifts.

It's so easy. Send no money now. Simply fill in the coupon below and post it to -
Reader Service, FREEPOST, PO Box 236, Croydon, Surrey CR9 9EL.

— NO STAMP REQUIRED —

Free Books Coupon

Yes! Please rush me 4 FREE Romances and 2 FREE gifts! Please also reserve me a Reader Service subscription. If I decide to subscribe I can look forward to receiving 6 brand new Romances for just £0.80 each month, postage and packing FREE. If I decide not to subscribe I shall write to you within 10 days - I can keep the free books and gifts whatever I choose. I may cancel or suspend my subscription at any time. I am over 18 years of age.

Ms/Mrs/Miss/Mr _____ EP56R

Address _____

_____

Postcode _____ Signature _____

mps
MAILING
PREFERENCE
SERVICE